Jay County Public Library
Portland, Indiana

W9-AXH-950

JMF   Christian, Mary Blount

        Deadline for danger

DISCARD

JAY COUNTY PUBLIC LIBRARY

1. Library materials are loaned for either 7 or 14 days and may be renewed once for the same period, so long as another patron has not requested that material.
2. A fine will be charged for each day kept overtime. No material will be issued to any person incurring such a fine until it has been paid.
3. Each borrower is responsible for all library materials drawn on his card and for all fines accuring on same.

DEADLINE FOR DANGER

Mary Blount Christian

Cover and frontispiece by Marie DeJohn

ALBERT WHITMAN & COMPANY, NILES, ILLINOIS

Jay County Public Library
Portland, Indiana

Library of Congress Cataloging in Publication Data

Christian, Mary Blount.
 Deadline for Danger.

 Summary: When Mike and Nita don't tell the truth about
skipping their journalism class, their deception takes
on a sinister life of its own.
 [1. Honesty—Fiction. 2. Journalism—Fiction]
I. DeJohn, Marie, ill. II. Title.
PZ7.C4528Db 1982   [Fic]   82-17470
ISBN 0-8075-1518-3

The text of this book is set in twelve point Baskerville.

Text © 1982 by Mary Blount Christian
Illustrations © 1982 by Marie DeJohn
Published in 1982 by Albert Whitman & Company, Niles, Illinois.
Published simultaneously in Canada by General Publishing, Limited, Toronto.
All rights reserved. Printed in the United States of America.

To Kathleen Tucker

CHAPTER ONE

"Don't be so nervous," Nita teased. "It's not the first time we ever had lunch off campus, you know."

Mike glanced at his watch between bites of his hamburger. "Exactly! It's *not* the first time. And we aren't seniors with off-campus privileges. One more cut and I'll be suspended. I could miss my mid-term tests. It would effect my grade point average and there goes college. Who'll hire a reporter who never went to college?"

Nita made a loud slurping noise as she struck bottom with her straw. "We don't look all that different from the seniors, do we? Even if one of the teachers spots us, how'll he know we're only juniors?"

"He'll know," Mike said. He tapped his watch and held it to his ear. "Oh, my gosh! It's stopped!"

He turned to the skinny, dark-haired boy leaning against the soft drink machine. "You got the time?" he asked.

"One-fifteen."

"We *are* late!" Mike said. He grabbed Nita's arm. "Come on, hurry!"

Nita pulled him back. "We'll be in a lot more trouble if we get caught in the halls during class without a permit. We might as well wait until the end of the period and go back when the halls are full of kids."

Mike slumped in agreement. "Yeah, you're right. We'd stand out in the empty halls like Bach at a rock concert. But what'll we tell Kroeger about missing journalism class?"

"You know how easy to fool he is. He probably didn't even call the class roll. Meet me at the lockers after school. We'll talk to Kroeger together." Nita patted Mike's arm, reassuring him. "Let me handle it, okay? I'll think of something by the end of the day."

"Yeah, well," Mike said, resigned. He leaned against the counter, gazing at his kooky friend. If you could overlook her crazy corkscrew hairdo and her smudged eye shadow, Nita was really a pretty girl.

But that imagination! She was good at making up stories. Of course, her story hadn't helped him the last time he'd cut class. He was always getting into trouble because of Nita. Why did he always listen to her? he wondered. Why didn't he just walk away and find his own brand of trouble?

When the bell rang at 1:50 for the class change, Nita and Mike were back at school. They scooted into the hall, joining the pushing, shoving students.

Mike didn't relax until he was safely tucked behind his too-small desk in American History. Mrs. Bates droned on about the War Between the States. He sighed, dreading the last bell when he and Nita would have to face Kroeger. He just hoped that the journalism teacher hadn't turned in the absentee slips. He and Nita would be in big trouble if the attendance office found out they'd been in every class but one.

After school Mike met Nita in the three-hundred hall. Together they entered Room 314. Mike knew outsiders viewed the journalism room — or J-room, as it was often called — as if it were the scene of weird pagan rites. But he, like the other journalism students, felt as if he belonged there more than any other place in school.

Knee-high stacks of newspapers from all over the country lined the faded walls. Brittle, yellowed clippings were tacked or taped on every available wall space, even the chalkboards. The sight of the clippings always quickened his pulse. Reporting for a newspaper — fighting deadlines, digging up facts that no one wanted to give you, kneading words together in a way that made sense — was all he'd ever wanted to do. He could barely wait to finish growing up!

Mike sniffed the familiar odors. Smells of oil and ink from the typewriters mingled with the odor of stale doughnuts. Days' old soft-drink cans cluttered the desks. Ever since Mr. Kroeger had given the school janitors "what for" when they threw out some of his favorite papers, the cleaning of this room had been left to the journalism staff.

The J-room was probably a fire inspector's nightmare, but Mike loved it, especially when the place was filled with the clatter of activity that preceded an edition of Travis High's bi-weekly school paper, the *Campus Caller*.

Rob Kroeger was bent over a stack of papers at his messy desk. When Mike and Nita approached, he brushed back his thinning strands of gray hair, patted his ample stomach, and greeted them.

"Missed you two in class this afternoon." He spoke casually, without judgment. "What happened?"

Mike opened his mouth to speak, but snapped it shut when Nita shot him a warning glance. Okay, Miss Smarty, he thought, *you* go ahead and handle it.

"We were at Pop's—" Nita said.

Oh, great, Mike thought. So far, she's telling the truth, which should get us something just short of a firing squad.

"Oh?" Mr. Kroeger said. His brows dipped into little checkmarks.

"—on a story," Nita continued, obviously undaunted. "We're—we're working on a story for the school paper and just let time get away from us."

"The story's so big it needs both of you?" Mr. Kroeger asked. He locked his fingers behind his neck and leaned back in his chair. "Tell me about it."

Mike was relieved that Mr. Kroeger seemed to be open to Nita's excuse—whatever it might be. Still Mike felt uneasy giving Nita's wild imagination a free hand in creating an alibi.

"It's going to take a lot of research," Nita said. "It's an exposé."

Mr. Kroeger's gray eyes danced behind the thick lenses of his glasses. Nita had said the magic word—exposé.

Mr. Kroeger often spent the entire period telling the class about daring stories he had written while he worked for one of the big Eastern dailies.

Mike realized his teacher must miss the excitement of reporting. Mr. Kroeger was obviously hooked by Nita's words. He was like a hound on the trail of a rabbit.

Mr. Kroeger leaned forward as if trying to savor every word. "Exposé," he repeated, as if he'd just tasted something delicious. "Of what?"

"I'd—that is, we'd—rather not say anything just yet," Nita said. "Not until we have a better handle on the story, that is."

"Don't you trust me?" Mr. Kroeger asked. He looked at them with a hurt expression. "Think of me as your managing editor. Reporters should trust their managing editors, don't you think?"

Mike held his breath, waiting for Nita's reply.

"Drugs," she said.

"Drugs?" Mr. Kroeger echoed. "You mean illegal drugs—here on campus?"

"Er, ah—yessir," Nita replied.

Mike realized he was still holding his breath. Drugs? Of all the dumb things to say. He let his breath out in a wheezing cough.

"Okay," Mr. Kroeger said. He suddenly took on the air of an editor Mike had seen on a TV show. He barked out orders. "Ask Clint to save some space on page one, just in case you get the story in time for the next issue. Get me a first draft by tomorrow—whatever you already have. Maybe—"

Mike could stand the tension no longer. So far, Kroeger wasn't asking the tough questions a teacher should ask. It sounded as if he wanted them to go ahead with the assignment!

"The story may turn out to be nothing," Mike said, surprised at the loudness of his own voice. "We can't be sure yet."

"True," Mr. Kroeger said, rubbing his chin in

thought. "Some stories don't pan out. But try! This could be a really big scoop, don't you think?"

Mike knew he had to get out of the J-room, or he would crack wide open. He pushed into the hall, leaving Nita with their teacher.

She followed in a minute and burst into a fit of giggles. "He even offered to let us out of class if we needed the time," she said. "We *did* it!"

"Nita, for crying out loud!" Mike yelled. "Are you crazy? Of all the stupid subjects to pull out of the air. Drugs! We don't know ANYTHING about them. And Mr. Kroeger expects us to write a newspaper article."

Nita shrugged off Mike's concern. "Everybody knows there are illegal drugs around here. The dailies called our campus one of the most involved in town — you read the story yourself. And you can spot stoned kids all the time. They may not cause trouble, but they sit in class like lumps, totally out of it. We can do some kind of story — don't worry!"

"But I do worry! *How* are we going to write a story?" Mike asked her.

Nita laughed. "The same way we got the idea. We'll make it up." She gave his cheek a friendly pinch. "I'm telling you, making up a story will be no trouble at all."

Mike scowled at her. "Trouble! I have a feeling we haven't even begun to see trouble yet."

CHAPTER TWO

"What can be the harm?" Nita asked. "I mean, we all know that some of the kids are on drugs. That's the truth. We can make up a hypothetical case—sort of mix some facts together. Plenty of TV dramas are done that way."

"I suppose we could read some medical reports to make the article sound authentic," Mike said. He paused. "What am I saying? This is crazy. We can't do it, Nita."

"Sure we can," she coaxed. "We won't name any names. We'll make the kids so ordinary they can't be recognized. Besides, the story will never see print. You know our principal watchdogs everything that goes in the paper. He'd never approve a story that throws a bad light on his dear old school, even if we wrote the most terrific piece of journalism ever."

Mike shook his head. "I just have an ugly feeling that we're getting into a lot more than we can handle, that's all."

"Don't be a coward," Nita said. "We'll fix it up so the kids sound anonymous. We'll say that all the names have been changed to protect the innocent. Only in this case, I guess it will be to protect the guilty—us." She giggled. "It'll be kind of fun, don't you think? I mean, I'll get to practice writing fiction. I like to make things up. Don't you ever want to write fiction?"

"Not really," Mike admitted. "YOU make it up." He grabbed his sweater from his locker and slammed the door shut. "I have a history report due tomorrow morning. See you."

The next morning Mike saw Nita before school. She was sipping a soda at Pop's.

"This would make a good meeting place, don't you think?" she said, glancing around the jammed store.

"Meeting place? For what?" Mike asked.

"Dope drops, silly!" she said. "Sometimes I can't believe you are so dense!"

Mike flushed at her teasing. "At least I don't have scrambled eggs for brains, like some people I know. What are you talking about, anyway?"

"For the story—our story. For Mr. Kroeger. I'm following the routine for writing a news piece. You tell who, what, when, where, why, and sometimes how. Pop's can be the where—the place the story happens."

Mike stared at her. "You really are crazy, Nita," he snapped. "You can't mention a real place like this! You don't know what you're getting into."

"Oh, I don't intend to mention Pop's. I just mean to describe it in a general way. All convenience stores look a lot alike, anyway. I'll give the place a phony name."

Mike bit his lip, thinking. "You mean, you'll mix up the description—describe this store and other stores, too—so nobody will know you're talking about Pop's?"

He felt a little easier. Maybe Nita's idea would work. They wouldn't be telling the truth, exactly, but then they wouldn't be lying, either. Drugs were around and lots of people used them. What was the harm in writing about them? Maybe the article would do some good.

And anyway, as Nita said, the story would never see print. The principal would see to that. They were just doing an exercise in reporting, not writing a real article for the paper.

In journalism class that day Mr. Kroeger seemed unusually cheery. Mike wondered if his teacher was thinking about his and Nita's hot scoop.

Mr. Kroeger whistled a nontune as he moved around the big conference table looking at the various articles and features the students had brought for what Mike called "journalism show-and-tell time."

"Maybe you'd better save some room in your page one dummy," Mr. Kroeger told Clint Morris, the editor-in-chief. He winked secretly at Mike.

Surely Kroeger didn't really intend to use the story! Mike's stomach churned. He turned to give Nita an accusing look. She shrugged innocently at him.

After school, Mike confronted Nita. "This thing has gone too far already. We can't go through with it."

"Don't worry," she told him. "Mr. Kroeger just likes the excitement. Would you rather go in and tell him we cut—and take the consequences?"

Mike bit his lip in thought. He needed every good grade he could get. He was struggling to be eligible for college without having to take the entry exams. He was so nervous about tests that he couldn't count on himself not to panic and flunk, even if he knew all the answers by heart.

And good grades didn't come when you had suspensions on your record. Teachers didn't take kindly to kids who cut. They remembered the cuts, and if there was any choice between giving a higher or lower grade, they gave a lower one.

Mike knew he had to get the best grades possible or he'd never make it to college—and to a newspaper job.

"Yeah, well," he agreed hesitantly.

"Now answer some questions," Nita said. "Play word association with me, okay?"

Mike sighed and nodded.

"Height."

Mike imagined himself fully grown and matured. "Tall," he said.

"Hair."

He looked at Nita's hair. "Blonde."

"Hair again."

"Wavy," he said with a grin.

"Hair again."

"Dark," he said, thinking of his own. "What are we doing? This doesn't make any sense at all."

"Of course it does!" Nita argued. "Just answer me—voice."

"Raspy," he replied, remembering the villain he'd seen on the late, late movie last weekend. "Now tell me what we're doing, or I'm through with the game."

Nita sighed wearily. "Okay. Listen to this. 'The tall, blonde boy with wavy hair and a raspy voice reached into the pocket of his designer jeans and pulled out a twenty-dollar bill. The second boy, who had short-cropped dark hair and was of average build, handed him a small packet of white powder. This reporter has reason to believe the packet contained cocaine. In the crowd of students pushing and shoving around the soft-drink machine in the small store, hardly anyone noticed the drug exchange except these two reporters for the *Campus Caller.*'"

Mike laughed. "That's the worst garbage I've ever

heard. Kroeger isn't going to buy it. It's pitiful."

Nita raised herself to her full five feet one-half inch, her left eyebrow somehow managing to peak higher than her right one. "Oh, yeah? Well, Mr. Pulitzer Prize, why don't you try your expert pen at the story? We'll just see who can write a more convincing piece!"

"Maybe I will," Mike snapped. "Not for print, of course. Just to show you that I can do it."

"You do that !" Nita growled. She stalked off in an indignant huff, her nose in the air.

Mike slapped his forehead. "Okay, Mr. Smart Guy," he scolded himself. "You've really done it now. You've let Nita goad you into a writing contest. How could you get into such a phony scheme, anyway?"

A little voice inside kept saying, "Stupid, stay away from this — you'll only get into trouble."

Mike knew he should listen to that little voice. But he had ignored little voices before. He knew he was going to ignore this one, too.

There was no way he could refuse Nita's challenge. He could write rings around her any day.

The contest was on now. His journalistic know-how was on the line. He had to go through with the story.

He had to show Nita.

CHAPTER THREE

At home that evening Mike finished his math, then pulled out the portable typewriter. Mr. Kroeger urged his students to get used to doing all their writing on the machine. He said they'd never have time to handwrite articles if they were up against publication deadlines.

"Okay," Mike told himself. "Now how did Nita do it? Word association, huh? Okay. Place? That stand of junipers behind the bleachers at the track field—yeah, that sounds like just the kind of place to have a secret meeting. Just far enough from the main school grounds."

"Who?" he asked himself aloud. "Maybe I ought to describe a kooky girl Nita's size and age. No, a guy. Maybe he should be wearing a school sweater—that way I could show he was definitely one of our students and not just someone passing by.

"What does the second guy have? A lid of grass? A few pills? I'll show Nita who's the real writer!"

Mike inserted the paper, set the margins, and tapped out his story.

A few minutes after school was dismissed this reporter observed what appeared to be a drug transaction on the campus of Travis High. An unidentified dark-haired male student wearing a school sweater and a second light-haired male student wearing a khaki jacket were spotted near the bleachers of the track field.

Hidden behind some juniper bushes, this reporter witnessed the student in the khaki jacket pass several packets of what appeared to be pot and a second unidentified substance to the male in the school sweater. The letterman then handed an undetermined number of bills to the second student.

Mike leaned back and read what he'd typed. "Not great, but not bad either," he told himself. "Not bad at all. I bet it beats Nita's story!"

He wrote that the reporter had witnessed a similar scene just blocks from the campus. He told about students who appeared to be high in the classrooms, although they offered no discipline problems.

The next day he and Nita rushed to see Mr. Kroeger after school. It had been their teacher's suggestion that they turn in their stories after school instead of in journalism class. That way he could keep their identities secret — for their own safety, he told them. That made Mike feel a bit uneasy. Safety? What did Mr. Kroeger mean?

"Let me see what you two have," Mr. Kroeger greeted them. "Separate stories, huh? Well, that's all right. You should work on combining them, though."

He hunched intently over the stories while Mike and Nita exchanged glances.

"A letterman?" Mr. Kroeger said. His eyes danced from the page to Mike. "This is good stuff so far. What you have is fine. Use it as the main story. Nita, maybe you can get some statistics from the police department to add to the article. Okay?"

Mike grinned at Nita as they left the classroom together. "He wants to use my story. I told you I could do it," he bragged.

"You are really crazy, Mike Bradshaw!" Nita snapped. "A letterman? Why didn't you just say the principal, for heaven's sake? A letterman? Good grief! The idea was to write descriptions of people no one would recognize. Everyone recognizes lettermen!"

Mike grimaced. "I guess I just got carried away. I never thought of that. Lettermen aren't exactly like weeds around here, are they? What do I do now?"

Nita shrugged. "The stuff is never going to be published, anyway. We're just doing exercises to please Mr. Kroeger."

"You're right, of course," Mike said, relieved. "But he is holding front-page space. What if he gets carried away?"

"Even if the article got all the way to galleys, Roland would never let it go to press. He's the principal and he's got final approval of everything."

Mike relaxed. "Yeah. I guess you're right. I wish we'd never got into this stupid mess, anyway. I feel like a nut!"

Nita laughed. "You write like one, too! Letterman, indeed! Should I get the research from the police department? Or do you think we could just stall until the deadline has passed?"

"Maybe we should stall," Mike said. "At least it's worth a try." Somehow he had the feeling that Mr. Kroeger was not to be put off, though.

He was right. The next day before class Mr. Kroeger handed Mike a stack of papers—pages and pages of police statistics. "It's going to be a fine story, kids," he told them. "It's a cinch to win the high-school journalism award."

He laughed. "I wonder if the Pulitzer has ever been given to a bi-weekly school paper?"

Mike met Nita after school. He waved the papers in front of her. "So much for stalling," he said. "What do you think our chances are for getting out of this scrape now?"

Nita shook her head. "Not much. Our only hope is that Roland will nix the whole thing." She grinned. "He will, of course! You know old Roland isn't going to admit that there's anything wrong on *his* campus."

Mike nodded. "Yeah, he'll never approve the story. Can you just see the furor it would cause if it was printed? The parents' organization, the school board— who wouldn't be after him?" He paused, savoring the image of angry parents lined up in the hall.

Nita laughed. "Yeah, and the football, track, and basketball teams would gang up in their letterman sweaters to get the finks that wrote the story!"

Mike felt a lump growing in his throat.

Well, the story would never see print. He hoped.

CHAPTER FOUR

All week Mike comforted himself with the thought that the principal would never allow the story to be printed. There had been plenty of times when Mr. Roland had killed a story that he felt would put the school in a bad light. He hated controversy.

Mike kept telling himself there was nothing to worry about. Nonetheless, the day the paper came out he could hardly eat breakfast. He and Nita hurried to school and grabbed the paper anxiously. What Mike saw made his stomach lurch.

"Letterman Seen Making Drug Deal," the headline read.

"My gosh!" he yelled at Nita. "I don't believe it! Roland could never have approved of this. What happened?"

Nita stared at the front page. "Well, at least Kroeger didn't print our real names. The editor's note at the top of the story says that all names, including the reporters', have been changed for everyone's protection."

"Yeah," Mike mumbled. "Maybe without real names nobody will pay any attention to the story. You think?"

Nita wasn't often shaken by anything. Her face was often hard to read, but today Mike detected worry lines around her mouth. He thought she didn't look any calmer than he felt.

Wherever he and Nita walked all day, they saw students huddled together with copies of the newspaper. The drug story was the main topic of conversation in the halls, classrooms, and lunchroom. Not even the cheerleader election seemed as interesting.

Mike and Nita cut short their lunch hour to talk with Mr. Kroeger. As they approached the J-room, Mike was alarmed to see a group of the varsity boys huddled outside the door.

"They're snarling and snapping like caged tigers," Nita observed.

Loud voices from inside the J-room carried into the hall.

"Every letterman is suspect now!" a deep, gravelly voice yelled. "I demand you tell me which of my boys is involved! I don't want any bad apples on my varsity tree."

Nita wrinkled her nose. "It's Coach Troy. Nobody else could sound so corny," she whispered to Mike.

He laughed in spite of himself.

"The identity of the reporters is confidential." The voice belonged to Mr. Kroeger, and it seemed surprisingly loud and strong. "Don't depend on the press to do your work for you, Troy!"

"Who wrote that story?" the coach yelled. "I want to talk to the kids myself."

"No way," Kroeger yelled. "Not even the principal knows their names. And that's the way it's going to stay."

Mike held his breath as the door burst open and Coach Troy brushed past them. The muttering crowd of sweater-clad boys closed ranks and followed their coach down the hall.

Mr. Kroeger pushed open the door. "Come in, come in," he said. He closed the door. He grinned at Mike and Nita. "I wanted to talk to you before class. I guess you saw the story, didn't you? Good play—right there in the number one spot."

"We saw," Mike said. "It was hard to miss. But I don't get it. How did Roland give his approval?"

Mr. Kroeger's eyebrows dipped over his lids. "I put my job on the line—that's how," he said.

Mike felt his heart catch in his throat. "What do you mean—your job on the line?"

Mr. Kroeger seemed to calm down some. His face

lost its pinkish tinge. He pulled a bottle from his desk drawer and shoved a couple of antacid tablets into his mouth before he spoke again. "I wasn't going to let him tell me no this time. The story's too important. Roland finally just washed his hands of it. He said if it caused a furor to forget that he ever discussed the matter with me. He said the burden was on my back."

"You shouldn't have done that, Mr. Kroeger," Mike said. "I wish you hadn't. You're taking too big a risk for just a story."

Nita grinned admiringly at Mr. Kroeger. "Wow. I can just picture you standing up to him. It's too bad we had to use phony names. I never had a lead story before."

Mike exploded at Nita. "Are you crazy? Look at this school now. Everybody in the journalism department is suspected of writing that story. Half my math class didn't even speak to me this morning. And they don't know I wrote it. They just know I work on the paper."

"Yeah," Nita agreed. "But nobody is speaking to anybody much, anyway. Every kid in school seems to think everyone else is pushing or buying or tattling. I had no idea the press could be so powerful!"

Mr. Kroeger grinned, nodding. "The press can make things better—if it's left alone to do its job."

Mike scowled at Nita. She seemed to forget the

whole story was a hoax. She couldn't think of anything but seeing her name in print.

"I think we should retract the story," Mike said.

Mr. Kroeger's grin slowly faded. "Retract? Why? It's all factually correct — isn't it? I mean, I went to the wire for this story. If it's not all correct I could lose my job. And you kids could lose your newspaper — for good."

Mike felt Nita's fingers dig into his arm as she spoke. "We just don't want to make trouble for anybody, that's all."

Mr. Kroeger scratched his chin as he looked studiously at their faces for what seemed like an eternity. Mike could feel himself crumbling inside.

"Reporters report," Mr. Kroeger said at last. "They don't make the world ugly. They only report the truth, which is sometimes ugly. That is just something we learn to live with. Newspapers aren't always popular, of course. There are still plenty of people who blame The *Washington Post* for Watergate."

Mr. Kroeger leaned back and rubbed his stomach gingerly. Mike suddenly remembered that his teacher had left the newspaper business because of ulcers. Maybe he hadn't learned to live with the pressure of being unpopular.

Mike slumped into his chair, feeling his knees growing weak beneath him. It wasn't only his grades and college at stake now. If he and Nita told anyone the story was phony, Mr. Kroeger could lose his job. Their teacher had put his job on the line because he trusted them. Could they pay back his trust by getting him fired? And it wasn't just Mr. Kroeger who would suffer, either. He'd said the students could lose the newspaper. That wouldn't make Mike or Nita particularly popular.

It was a few minutes before the rest of the journalism students made their way into the room. Part of the period was spent going over stories others had written for the next edition. The class voted on the stories that should run.

"I think we should do a follow-up on the drug piece," the editor said.

"But Clint!" Nita argued. "In two weeks it'll be old news. The home ec department has two students in the cook-off finals. I think — "

"All who think we should continue the drug stories say aye," Clint said.

To Mike's dismay it was unanimous that the story about drugs on campus should be followed up with another drug story.

After class Nita asked Mike, "If you didn't agree, why did you vote for it?"

"For the same reason you did," he said. "If I didn't, everybody would have known I was one of the two reporters. And they would've figured out who the other one was in no time. Tweedle Dum and Tweedle Dee—that's us."

"Yeah," Nita agreed.

"And even though Mr. Kroeger hasn't told the rest of the journalism class who wrote the story, I get the ugly feeling that everybody knows."

"Maybe you're just being paranoid," Nita said as they ambled down the hall to their next class.

Mike grabbed Nita's arm. His heart skipped a beat. "Let's hope you are right. But do you see what I see?"

Two men in three-piece gray suits walked toward the J-room, making their way through the crowds of students.

"Cops," Mike said. "Narcs." There was no mistaking them.

He and Nita stared, frozen in place, as the two men headed straight for Room 314.

Mike felt sure about the purpose of their visit. "They're here about the story," he whispered to Nita. "I just know it! Now what are we going to do?"

CHAPTER FIVE

When the men had entered the J-room, Mike and Nita strolled casually past and peered through the glass panel on the door.

"I was right," Mike said grimly. "Look. That shorter guy just shoved his open wallet toward Kroeger. I'm sure he is showing his ID. Now what?"

"Don't panic," Nita said. "Maybe they are here for something entirely different — maybe they want publicity about something in the school paper."

"Do you really believe that?" Mike asked.

"Not really. If only we could hear what — I've got it! Come on," she said grabbing his arm.

Pulling Mike behind her, she slipped into the empty home economics room next to the journalism room. "No one's here this period," she explained. Nita pulled two water glasses from the cabinet and ran water over their open edges.

"This is it?" Mike asked disgustedly. "You want a drink? How does that solve anything?"

"No, silly," she said, grinning. "Didn't you ever

eavesdrop as a kid? Didn't you ever use a glass as a sound conductor against a wall? What a sheltered life you've led!"

She turned the wet edge against the wall between the two classrooms and placed her ear against the flat bottom of the glass. "Shhhh," she hissed.

Mike frowned at her. "Hear anything?"

She nodded and put her finger to her lips, silencing him. Mike shrugged and placed his glass against the wall, too.

". . . you think you are, anyway?" It was Kroeger's voice growing shriller than Mike'd ever heard it before. "You don't have any right to ask details my reporters have uncovered. If you want any more information, you can subscribe to the school paper. If my student reporters can uncover facts, so can you."

"Mr. Kroeger," another voice said, "the courts are still debating the question of confidentiality. Not everyone believes you have the right to protect your sources. And we need your help now. All we're asking are some names—just something to go on. We've been trying to crack this campus drug ring for some time now. Nothing we've tried has given us much success."

"And what have you tried?"

"Never mind," a third voice interrupted. "Why not give your reporters the opportunity to decide for

31

themselves if they want to help us? Just give us their names and we'll ask them, okay?"

Mike felt a familiar lump growing in his throat. "What if Kroeger tells them our names? What'll they do to us?" he asked Nita.

She scowled, silencing him.

The second voice spoke again. "Look, we can do this the hard way—we can—"

Suddenly the door to the home ec room burst open, and Ms. Hedricks, the home economics teacher, whirled in. "What are you two doing in here? Why do you have those glasses against the wall?" she sputtered.

Mike jumped, nearly dropping the glass. "I—I—" he struggled to find an explanation.

Nita smiled at Ms. Hedricks, then turned slowly and deliberately to Mike. "No, Mike. I think you must be wrong. I don't hear any termites in the wall." She casually took the glasses to the sink and rinsed them. She wiped them with the dishcloth that hung on the nearby rack and replaced them in the cabinet. She smiled again at Ms. Hedricks. Then she casually grabbed Mike's hand and strolled from the room.

Mike could feel Ms. Hedricks' eyes burning into his back. "Kids," he heard her mumble. "They're all crazy. But especially those journalism kids!"

"Termites!" Mike headed toward the journalism

door. "Sometimes I don't think you're for real, Nita."

The men were gone when they looked through the glass panel. Mike and Nita went inside. "Were those narcs who just left here?" Mike asked.

Mr. Kroeger sat rubbing his stomach. "They did appear a bit obvious, didn't they?"

"Can they make you tell our names?" Mike asked.

Mr. Kroeger chuckled appreciatively. "I won't even ask how you heard our conversation—you probably did some good snooping. No, they can't make me talk. Not even Principal Roland knows your names. So that keeps you safe from any pressure that might develop."

Mike felt chilled. "Pressure?" he echoed. "What kind of pressure?"

"Don't worry—it'll never happen," Mr. Kroeger assured him.

"You mean pressure like in that case I read about where a judge tried to get a reporter to tell his source?" Nita asked.

"Something like that. But don't worry," Mr. Kroeger assured them once more.

Mike and Nita hurried to their next classes. They met again after school. Mike was beginning to feel as if things were closing in. How could one silly prank endanger a man's job, maybe cause a whole school to lose its newspaper, and get the cops so uptight?

33

"I think we should confess," Mike said. "We should tell Mr. Kroeger we made the story up."

"We can't. We're in too deep. You heard him. If it gets out that the story was a hoax, we could lose the newspaper. And he could lose his job!"

"Are you sure you aren't just concerned about yourself — about getting suspended?" Mike accused her.

Nita laughed. "Since when have you ever seen me concerned for myself? You're always telling me I'm not concerned enough for the consequences of my actions. And now that I am, you still aren't satisfied!"

Mike searched her face for some clue as to Nita's real feelings. Was she really concerned for Mr. Kroeger and the school paper? Was he being selfish, wanting to clear his conscience by telling the truth? "You don't think the police will call Kroeger to court to testify about his sources? I heard about that happening to a publisher once."

"Nobody's going to get that involved in a high school newspaper," Nita assured him. "The best thing we can do is keep quiet. The storm will blow over."

Mike hoped Nita was right. "I can't believe I went along with this scam. I wish I'd taken a suspension for cutting class and gotten my punishment over with."

He walked Nita to her home, a two-story brick house that covered nearly half a block. He paused at the gate, feeling, as usual, a twinge of embarrassment. In all the years he'd known Nita she'd never invited him in. "The place is so full of valuable antiques that my grandmother doesn't want my friends in. Sorry," she'd explained once when he'd asked to come inside.

Nita was like that princess in the ivory tower — what was her name — Rapunzel? But was her grandmother really playing the role of the wicked witch? Or had Nita chosen to isolate herself? Mike wondered. Was there some reason she didn't want any of her friends to come in?

He had never tried to visit her again. He still felt hurt though, every time he came to the gate.

He gazed up at the structure enviously, thinking for a moment of his own crowded house. No wonder Nita didn't seem concerned about school and grades. If she did decide to go to college, her family could pay her way easily. Who knows? Maybe her grandmother could buy her a newspaper, too!

His own worries flooded back over him. "Do you remember how that court case came out with the publisher who refused to reveal his source?" he asked Nita.

"No, how?" she asked, slipping through the wrought iron gate and shutting it with a clink.

"He went to jail," Mike said.

CHAPTER SIX

Mike had trouble sleeping that night. He kept wondering if maybe he and Nita shouldn't just confess to Kroeger that they'd only made up the stories so they wouldn't be in trouble for cutting class. Maybe they should take their punishment and get it over with.

Making up the stories had seemed like such a harmless prank in the beginning. But detectives coming to school—that was something different. And so many people were involved now. So many could be hurt! Mr. Kroeger could lose his job. The school could lose its newspaper. And heaven knew how much trouble the school lettermen were in, with everyone suspecting them of being involved with drugs.

He rolled into a tight ball and pulled the covers to his chin. Mike knew he had to get Nita to agree before he could tell Kroeger. He couldn't just tell on himself without involving her, too. Maybe he could convince her to go with him to Kroeger and tell the truth. Later they could go to the principal and plead with him for their journalism teacher's job. They could convince Roland that Mr. Kroeger had been fooled like everyone else.

But would the police believe that the exposé had been just a prank? They might think Mike and Nita were denying everything to protect someone.

Maybe Nita was right. Maybe he should just keep quiet. Maybe he should, again, take her advice.

Mike sighed wearily. Nita had a wild imagination and he willingly followed her down any dark path she chose. It had been like that since they were kids. His mother generously called him "flexible." Sometimes he figured he was just plain wishy-washy—a pushover for Nita's dumb schemes.

Why did he put up with her all this time? he wondered angrily. Probably because of her imagination. She was always making up stories that involved him as a hero, stories that made him feel great. She'd make her tales sound so real that he believed he could do all sorts of amazing things. If it hadn't been for Nita, he'd never have imagined himself as a reporter for a newspaper. Maybe that was her appeal. She could open doors for him—doors that had been closed, even in his imagination.

He pushed himself to a sitting position and fluffed his pillow. Why did Nita want to shut him out of her home life? Was there that much difference in their lifestyles? She didn't dress any better than anybody else. Why was she so exclusive? So what if she did live in a mansion? Was her grandmother some kind of snob?

Mike lay watching the sky turn from black velvet to purple to green and finally to aquamarine as the sun climbed up over the horizon. He got up, groggy, when the alarm rang. He had no answers.

At school he joined the pushing, shoving mix of students in the main hall. He made his way to his locker, spun the combination lock, and pulled the door open.

His eyes fell on a piece of notebook paper taped on the edge of the shelf. Words sprawled across it in red. "Narcs Pay The Price Eventually! Beware!"

It was as if the blood left his head. He clutched the wall to balance himself. Someone had gotten into his locker! Someone had guessed he was one of the reporters.

He glanced around. No one seemed to be paying any attention to him. Who had done this? And what did the person mean, "Narcs Pay The Price"?

Someone touched his shoulder and Mike whirled around. He let out a long sigh. It was Nita.

"You, too?" She held a crumpled piece of notebook paper covered with the same sprawling print. "What does it mean?" she asked.

"I don't even want to think," he admitted. "I'm scared and I'm tired. Don't say anything, hear? We'll talk to Mr. Kroeger as soon as we can."

Nita nodded agreement. But her lower lip trembled. Seeing her crumble, even a little, Mike couldn't help but feel that things were worse than he thought. It would've been more comforting if Nita was her usual cool self.

The whole experience seemed like a nightmare—one of those dreams in which he had no control over himself or anything around him. He felt as if he were moving in glue.

The rest of the morning nobody seemed to notice him. But Mike still felt as if someone might be watching him. In his math class, he cautiously scanned the room from behind his algebra book. Who had written the note? Was it that lanky kid—what's his name?—in the coveralls who never seemed to pay any attention to anything? Or the girl falling asleep—the one who looked as if she was on something? Or—

At last the bell rang for journalism class. Mike hurried there and slid into his chair next to Nita. The room buzzed with whisperings.

Every journalism student had found a similar note in his locker.

Mr. Kroeger leaned forward and whispered to Mike and Nita. "Be thankful that you weren't omitted or singled out," he said. "You're still part of the crowd. Everyone in class is tarred with the same brush."

He straightened up and walked slowly around the conference desk as he spoke. "Don't worry," he told the class. "You don't have to be concerned about sneaks like this who leave anonymous notes. Start worrying when nobody complains. That means you aren't doing your job as reporters. The best compliment you can get is when *both* sides complain that you are reporting unfairly. That's when you can be sure you are the most accurate."

Mike felt better—but only a little—when he left class. At least he and Nita hadn't been singled out. It looked as if no one suspected them more than the other journalism students. But it made him uneasy to think that his combination lock had been opened and his locker had been gone through.

Where did the creep get the names of all the journalism students who were working in the paper? How did he know where the lockers were? And more important, how did he know the combinations of twelve people?

"It must have been someone who has access to the school records," Nita said. "Maybe one of the student helpers who works in the office. It's easy to get into the cabinets—the secretaries aren't fussy about keeping them locked. All those locker numbers are part of our permanent files here along with medical records and—"

"And home addresses," Mike added, feeling suddenly vulnerable. What if someone was angry—or scared—enough to try something violent? But the story wasn't real, he told himself. How could something made up threaten a real person?

Had something in the story made someone—someone who was really involved with drugs—think the newspaper reporters knew something more than was in the article? What might that person do if he really felt threatened?

CHAPTER SEVEN

When Mike got up the next morning, he checked the dark sagging circles under his eyes. After a second restless night, he looked like a zombie in a horror movie.

On impulse he walked to Nita's, intent on walking her to school. Before he'd made it through the iron gate, she came around the side of the mansion.

She looked cheerful and enthusiastic. "What would you say if I told you we could get a genuine interview with a real kid on drugs?" Nita asked him.

Mike searched her face. As usual, it was hard for him to tell if Nita was kidding. "I'd say you were making up another story. And if you're not, forget it," he snapped. "I don't believe you can get an interview, and besides, if you keep this up, you are going to get us expelled, or killed, or both. Remember those notes in our lockers? Somebody compared us to narcs."

"Don't be angry, Mike," Nita told him. "Didn't you read the paper this morning? I'm not sure the incident described in the front-page story is related to dope, but I'm willing to bet it is."

Mike felt his breath catch. "What happened?"

"A guy—one of our students—was found unconscious last night, in that vacant lot across from campus. You know that lot's a hangout for kids buying and selling drugs."

"Unconscious!" Mike echoed. "Was he hurt bad? Did he overdose, or what?"

"He was beaten," Nita said.

"Gosh!" Mike said. "Is he going to be all right?"

Nita shrugged. "I don't know. Maybe. The cops didn't tell the reporters much, according to the story. Maybe Mr. Kroeger will let us interview the victim at the hospital. Don't you think that would make a good story? Maybe we can get him to tell us he was involved in dope. That would be our first real lead."

"I'd like to know what happened, but I don't want anything to do with interviewing the victim," Mike said.

When he and Nita reached campus, they saw a crowd of students in the lot across the street. "I'll bet that's where they found the guy," Mike said.

"I've seen kids over there sometimes, passing a marijuana cigarette back and forth," Nita said.

"The weeds look pretty tall," Mike said. "What if nobody had found him? What if—" he shuddered.

The school bell rang, and students scrambled toward the central doors of the building. Mike followed them in, torn between wanting to follow up on the story and wanting to never hear anything about it again.

Later that day Mr. Kroeger shuffled papers on his desk and whistled a nontune as the students ambled in for their journalism class.

He pushed himself from the desk when the tardy bell sounded.

"When violence is done to one of our students, it's news," he said. "When it happens within view of our campus it is especially worthy news. I want us to cover this story to the best of our ability. And I think because you, as students, may have access to information outsiders may not have, we can do a fine job."

He sighed and rubbed his stomach gingerly. "Nita, you work in the office sixth period, don't you? Will you pull the victim's file and get some information about him? Get as much as you can—home address, parents' names, absentee record—anything you can dig up that might be useful." He paused. "And, er, be discreet."

A caution bell sounded in Mike's head. "Mr. Kroeger, is that all right? I mean, the records are private—"

"The public has a right to know," Mr. Kroeger assured him. "Besides, Nita works in the office. She isn't breaking in, or doing anything she doesn't do every day—right, Nita?"

44

Nita shrugged casually. "Right—I guess."

Mr. Kroeger turned to Mike. "You do the interview."

"Interview? What interview?"

"With the victim," Mr. Kroeger said patiently. "Find out anything and everything you can. Get some quotes we can use—need I say, good ones? I want to know exactly what happened—who his attackers were, why he thinks they were after him.

"I think it's time for this school paper to put out a special edition," he said. He paused, listening to murmurs of appreciation from the students. "I've already talked to our printers. They're willing. We have the funds earned from that special senior class edition. We want to hit the halls with this story while it's fresh. The *Campus Caller* is going to be a REAL newspaper."

Mr. Kroeger's face was flushed. His eyes sparkled with pleasure as he barked out his orders.

"But what about those warnings in the lockers?" Mike asked."What if somebody doesn't like what we're doing?"

Mr. Kroeger narrowed his eyes at Mike. He looked from one student to the other. "If any of you want out of journalism class, say so right now and I'll have you transferred to Study Hall. No questions asked. But stay and you'll have the opportunity to do something really good. You'll have a memorable experience to describe when you go job hunting one of these days, or when you try for scholarships to college."

The bell rang and the journalism students rushed toward the door. Nobody stopped by Kroeger's desk to ask for a transfer, Mike noticed. But nobody looked too eager to become a star reporter, either.

Mike hung back until the others had gone. "What if I can't get into the hospital to see this"—he glanced at the clipping to refresh his memory—"Jerry Cranford?"

"You can get in—just use your imagination," Mr. Kroeger offered, a smile playing across his pudgy face. "Why, I remember one time when I was trying to get into the bank files and I—"

"I've got to get to class, sir," Mike interrupted. "I'd like to hear that story some other time, of course." He hurried out the door before Mr. Kroeger could reply.

Nita was waiting in the hall. She eyed Mike huffily. "I don't see why he didn't let me do the interview," she complained. "I wouldn't have any trouble getting in to see that guy. Well, maybe the records will tell us something." She scooted off without waiting for Mike.

He made his way to his next class, muttering, "Use my imagination, Mr. Kroeger says. That's what got me into this mess in the first place."

CHAPTER EIGHT

Mike didn't wait for Nita after school. He knew he probably needed the information she'd get from the office files to have a really good interview with the beating victim. But he dreaded talking with the guy so much, he thought it'd be best to just get it over with — as quickly as possible.

On the way to the hospital, Mike wondered what he could say to the parents of the boy, if he saw them there. He remembered how scared his mother and dad had been whenever he or one of his brothers had been hurt. And nothing very serious had ever happened to them — nothing like being beaten up.

He wondered what to expect. He'd only seen crime victims on TV or in the movies, but he'd always known those cuts and bruises were created by makeup. He dreaded seeing someone who'd really been hurt.

He stopped at the main desk to ask directions. "Are you family?" the receptionist asked. "Only family is allowed in."

Mike took a deep breath and lied. "His brother." The words nearly choked him and he wished Nita was with him. She could tell stories to get out of tight squeezes without even sweating.

The receptionist gave Mike the room number. He rode the elevator to the third floor. Even numbers to the left, odd numbers to the right, the sign in the hall said. Mike turned left and froze on the spot.

A uniformed officer was sitting in a straight-back chair about mid-hall. He looked as if he was right outside Room 412, the room that would be Jerry Cranford's. Why was the cop there? Was he guarding Cranford? Did the police think Cranford was still in danger?

Mike bit his lip, thinking. How could he get into Cranford's room without the officer stopping him?

Mr. Kroeger had said to use his imagination. How could he fake his way in? Maybe he could go into the room next to Cranford's, pretending to be a visitor there. If the patients in the two rooms shared an adjoining bathroom, he might be able to go through the bathroom into Cranford's room. But what if the patient next to Cranford didn't want him coming through? What if he yelled?

Mike retreated toward the elevator to think. Spotting a linen supply room, he had an idea.

He glanced in both directions. No one was watching. He slipped inside the walk-in closet. It was lined with sheets, blankets, towels, and just what he was looking for — the hospital smocks the orderlies wore.

Mike put on a smock and a surgical cap. He decided not to wear a surgical mask. That might look too phony. He grabbed a stack of towels and sheets.

He paused to take a deep breath, then walked briskly down the hall. He didn't want to go directly to Cranford's room. That'd look too suspicious.

He pushed the door to Room 410 open first. Luckily that patient was alone and sleeping. Mike swung out of 410 whistling softly, nodded to the officer, and forced a smile. The officer nodded and continued reading his paper.

A woman leaned against the wall nearby. Her eyes were swollen and red. Her makeup was streaked and Mike could see the path of her recent tears. Was she the boy's mother? Mike wondered. She looked scared and unsure. Mike felt a pang of guilt for what he was about to do. He shook it off. He was trying to find out the truth. Wasn't that important?

Mike slipped inside room 412. The room smelled of disinfectant and roses. He pulled out his notebook from between two towels and eased over to the bedside. He stared at the swollen and bruised face of Jerry Cranford.

The guy's eyes were swollen nearly shut, the lids varying shades of blue and purple. Both of his lips were split and swollen. Fresh surgical stitches were visible.

Sprigs of sandy blond hair pushed through his head bandage. His hands and chest were also bandaged. He must've put up a real fight, Mike thought, nausea sweeping over him.

The stubble of whiskers on Jerry Cranford made him look old—older than Mike was. But it was hard to tell someone's age from his beard, Mike knew. Lots of guys his age had thicker whiskers than he did.

Mike leaned forward. "Jerry," he whispered. "Jerry Cranford. Can you hear me?"

The boy groaned and blinked, wincing as he tried to peer through his swollen lids.

"Who—who are you? How did you get in here?" He groped for the paging button on an electrical cord that was looped over the bed railing.

Mike gently pushed his hand away. "Please don't call the nurse. I won't stay long. I—I promise. I'm a reporter from the school paper. I just want to ask you a few questions, that's all."

"No—no. I can't tell you anything. I'll call Jake in. You better go—now!"

Jake must be the cop outside the door, Mike figured. He nodded. "Okay, I'll go. But first, can you tell me why someone would do this to you? Did you recognize who beat you up?"

"G-get out of here!" Jerry Cranford ordered. "Unless you'd like to be arrested, just get out."

"Can I talk to your parents, then? Let me just talk to them—you know, get a little more information about you."

"Jake!" Jerry Cranford yelled. "Jake!"

Mike dashed into the bathroom. He locked the door just as the officer answered Cranford's call. Was there another door in the bathroom, a door leading to the next room? There was. A khaki army jacket hung on its knob.

Mike scurried through the adjoining room, to the astonishment of the patient, who was awake. He ran out into the hall, peeling the smock and cap off as he ran. He could hear the cop banging on the bathroom door, yelling.

Mike didn't stop until he'd dumped the smock and linens in the linen closet. By the time the officer came out of Cranford's room, Mike looked like any other visitor in the hall.

He hurried outside. He couldn't get the smell of the hospital out of his nose. It made him dizzy and sick to his stomach. Or did his nausea come from the realization of what he'd done—ignoring hospital rules to break in on someone in pain? There must be a better way to get a story! What if he'd endangered Cranford's life somehow?

There was something about Jerry Cranford that made Mike feel even more uneasy. Cranford's sandy hair, his khaki jacket—they reminded Mike of someone. Suddenly he knew who it was—one of the imaginary students he had described in the phony story! *A second light-haired student wearing a khaki jacket,* he had written. Mike knew he would never forget that description. He'd probably never forget even one word of that dumb article.

Maybe it was an extraordinary coincidence, but Jerry Cranford did look like one of the people Mike had made up.

Was it somehow his fault that Jerry Cranford was lying in the hospital? Had Cranford been beaten up because of the article?

Mike didn't have Nita's phone number. She'd never given it to him. She said her grandmother didn't want her to give out an unlisted number. Still, he knew he had to tell her. He felt this news was something Nita should know. And he couldn't keep it to himself.

He pedaled as fast as he could. "Rapunzel, Rapunzel, let down your hair," he repeated to himself as he pedaled. He just hoped the princess was at home in her ivory tower. Maybe this news was the password that would get him inside her castle for the first time.

She was outside the gate. "I thought you might come by," she said. "How did it go?"

"I snuck in to see the victim," he said, disgusted. "You'd have been proud of me, Nita. I was as clever as you'd have been. But there was a cop outside the guy's room. And Cranford wouldn't tell me a thing."

Nita folded her arms smugly. "In a way I got nothing, too. But put our two nothings together and we may have something."

Mike made a face at her. "What's that supposed to mean? You're sounding screwier all the time."

Nita grinned. "Well, you know I was going to take a look at Jerry Cranford's school record. I took down his address. Then I decided I'd stop off at his house and get a photo of him for the paper. And—" she paused— "and the address on his records is a phony. There's a dry cleaners at that street number!"

"Maybe it's one of those family businesses. Maybe the Cranfords live above the cleaners," Mike offered.

"No way. I went inside and asked around. Nobody'd ever heard of Jerry Cranford."

"Maybe he gave a phony address so he could go to school in our district. Some kids have been caught do-ing that."

Nita shook her head. "The phony address made me suspicious about the rest of the information. His card said he'd transferred from Davis High. But I called their registrar pretending we needed his transcript, and they said they never heard of Jerry Cranford."

Mike let out his breath in a slow whistle. "A student who doesn't live anywhere and never went to school—Nita, what are we on to here?"

She laughed nervously. "I'm not sure. But I guess we'd better tell Mr. Kroeger what we have, huh?"

Mike frowned. If there was one thing he didn't want, it was to be pushed by Kroeger into writing another story. "I don't think so—at least not yet. Not until we have a bit more evidence. You know, that guy looked older than the rest of us to me. I wonder if he might be only pretending to be a student for some reason."

"Why would anyone go to school if he didn't have to?" Nita asked. "You think maybe Cranford is some kind of dope dealer just there for contacts?"

"I don't understand what he's doing either, but the police are protecting him. Why else would that cop have been outside his room? Maybe he's under arrest. But why wouldn't the paper have said that?"

"All we know right now is that Cranford's not a student—not a real one," Nita said. "But who is he? Maybe if we knew that, we'd have a lot of answers."

Mike leaned closer to Nita. "Something else is bothering me. That guy, whoever he is, looked a lot like the student I wrote about — the one who wore the khaki jacket and sold drugs to the letterman. I even saw a khaki jacket in the hospital bathroom. I get the ugly feeling that it's my fault Cranford's lying there in the hospital. Someone may *think* he's a drug dealer because of my story."

Nita grabbed Mike's arm and looked straight into his eyes. "You don't know that for sure — not until we find some more answers."

"Nita, we've got to be careful. Look at what happened to Jerry Cranford — whoever he is. What if something like that — or worse — happens to us?"

Mike thought he could see a flicker of raw fear in her eyes. Or was it only his own fear reflected there?

CHAPTER NINE

"We may have accidentally stumbled onto a real story," Mike told Nita. "Somebody thinks we know more than we really do. And that might be just as dangerous as if we *did* know something. It was dangerous for the guy in the hospital—whoever he is."

"We should tell Kroeger. He can advise us, don't you think?" Nita asked anxiously.

"Tell him what? That a boy whose identity we don't know was beaten up by we don't know whom? And that we have no idea why? I think we ought to get more information. Besides," Mike added bitterly, "I'm not so sure that Kroeger is the best one to ask for advice. Look where we are now, because of his advice!"

Nita gave a reluctant nod. "Let's hold off a little, then," she agreed. "Let's ask some discreet questions around school and see if anyone knows anything about this guy."

She smiled lightly. "Maybe there's some foul-up in

his records. Maybe he's just come out of reform school. Maybe he's one of those kids whose parents are in that federal protection program — you know, for being witnesses in crimes."

Mike nodded grimly. He knew there were a dozen possible explanations for the false information on Jerry Cranford's school record. But somehow he had the ugly feeling that Jerry Cranford had been beaten up because of the silly prank he and Nita had played.

At school the next day he and Nita did ask around. They found that nobody knew much about Jerry Cranford.

"I flirted a lot with him — he's cute!" Sally Flint admitted to Mike. "But he wouldn't tumble. I think maybe he's got a girl friend at another school."

At noon Nita reported that most of the students she talked to said Jerry was friendly, but he didn't ever give out any information about himself.

"I wouldn't tell you nothing!" one of the boys told Mike after lunch. "Even if I knew something I wouldn't tell a snoopy journalism student. Because of that drug story I got my curfew cut an hour short every night — just 'cause I go to school here. I'd like to get my hands on the creeps who wrote the story!"

Mike backed off. "Me, too, Pal. We all have to pay for a few, right?"

"Whew!" he breathed as he joined Nita. They exchanged their interview notes as they walked toward journalism class.

"Nothing but angry kids everywhere," Nita said. "Even the straight kids hate the idea of the story. If we find out anything it'll be by digging."

Mike opened the door to the journalism room.

"What happened?" Nita gasped.

The room was in shambles. Pieces of typewriters were lying around. They looked as if they'd been twisted by some giant hand. Stacks of newspapers had been shredded and strewn over the floor.

Sprawled across the chalkboard in red paint was a fresh message: "Stop snooping."

"When did this happen?" Mike said.

"I found the place this way this morning," Mr. Kroeger told them. "I think our little paper has stirred up a hornet's nest." He grinned. "We're on the right trail, Mike, Nita. We must be getting close. And if this is the worst they can sting in retaliation—"

Mike wasn't sure whether it was the sight of the destruction or the almost buoyant attitude of his teacher that upset him more. "I have a feeling it isn't," Mike interrupted. "I think that guy in the hospital got stung worse than this."

"You found out the guy is connected with your

story?" Mr. Kroeger asked eagerly. He reached into his desk and pulled out a couple of pink tablets, then popped them into his mouth.

"Not yet," Mike admitted. "We're working on it."

"Before I forget, you two meet me after school. I have some source material in my car I'd like for you to use in your next story. Good background on the national problem of drugs in the schools."

The class helped clean up the mess as best they could.

Mike and Nita attended their last classes before meeting Mr. Kroeger in the parking lot.

"That red coupe over th—" Mr. Kroeger said, pausing to gasp. "What—"

Mike looked at Mr. Kroeger's car and felt the hair on his neck prickle. All four tires were flat—slashed. The fenders had been kicked in. The doors had been battered. And carved into the paint were what looked like knife scars. Someone had vented a lot of hate and anger on the little car.

Mr. Kroeger stared, his jawline sagging, his shoulders stooped. He stood there a long time, saying nothing, rubbing his stomach. He fished through his pockets and extracted a set of keys and his antacid tablets. He popped a couple in his mouth, chewing slowly, still staring at the car.

He looked weary when he turned toward Mike and handed him a set of keys. "Would you get the camera from the locked cabinet in the J-room? I'd like pictures of the car before it's disturbed, please."

Grimly Mike nodded. He took the keys from Mr. Kroeger's trembling hands and ran back toward the school building. He paused long enough to ask the school secretary to call campus security and tell them briefly what had happened.

While it was unlikely that the police would rush to investigate a case of school parking lot vandalism, Mike asked her to report it to the city dispatcher, as well.

In the journalism room he checked to see that the camera was loaded with film, then he hurried back to the parking lot. He took pictures from every angle — wide shots to show that all the tires were flat, closeups to show the slashmarks and the dented fenders. Finished, he turned to see a uniformed officer approaching.

"Rob Kroeger?" the officer said. "Mr. Rob Kroeger of 999 West Dodd Avenue?"

Mr. Kroeger nodded. "I didn't expect such a response to vandalism," he said, extending his pudgy hand in greeting.

The officer shoved a folded paper toward Mr. Kroeger's extended hand. "Vandalism? That's too bad. You should really report that, sir."

Mr. Kroeger stared at the paper, his hand still extended.

It was a subpoena to appear in Judge Benderthorp's court.

"Subpoena for what?" Mike demanded to know.

Mr. Kroeger let his hand fall to his side. "Ah, Mike, Nita. So it begins. I'm afraid this has something to do with our story. Somebody wants names."

Nita grabbed Mike's arm as if to steady herself. He glanced at her, then at Mr. Kroeger.

They were caught in between the justice system and the criminals.

And both sides were closing in — fast.

CHAPTER TEN

The next morning Mike sat in his family's breakfast nook, staring at his oatmeal and toast. The food tasted like concrete. The washing machine jammed into one corner of the small kitchen chugged continuously.

"Problems, Mike?" his mother said as she poured her coffee and sat across from him. "Want to talk?"

He jumped at the sound of her voice. "Huh? Thanks, Mom, but I don't—"

"I hope you aren't thinking about a job after school again, Mike, because I just won't hear of it," his mother interrupted. "We've been through all this before. Of course, it's tough putting your brothers through college and grad school. But we're managing all right, what with staying in this house instead of moving to someplace more—comfortable."

"Mom—"

She silenced him with a wave of her hand. "If you had a job after school you couldn't work on the school newspaper. That's important to you. And the experience might help you get a good scholarship into a good journalism college. You won't need money then, anyway." She laughed lightly. "By that time maybe your brothers—*Doctor* Joe Bradshaw or *His Honor* Jerry Bradshaw can pay us back some of our college investment so we can help you."

The word *scholarship* was like a hit between the eyes to Mike. If he didn't get himself out of this crazy mess there would be no scholarship, no college, no journalism degree.

"Have you ever heard of Judge Benderthorp?" Mike asked aloud. He wanted to find out something about the judge who was to hear Kroeger's case.

"Oh, social studies research, huh?" his mother replied, nodding. "I remember reading something about him recently in the papers. Seems he tossed a bunch of reporters out of his court room and they filed suit against him—something about freedom of information. Some call him the 'hanging judge'—as a joke, of course. They haven't hanged anyone in this state in decades." She laughed lightly.

Mike didn't see any humor in the judge's nickname. "He's really tough?" he asked.

"I suppose you could say that. I read he'd had some kind of personal tragedy that's supposed to make his patience wear thin with criminals and with reporters he thinks are protecting them by withholding their sources." She glanced at her watch. "Oops, I'm late." She shoved her dishes into the sink, gave Mike a quick peck on the cheek, and dashed out the door.

Mike worried that the 'hanging judge' might not be sympathetic to the cause of school journalism. He wondered if Mr. Kroeger was worried. But he was surprised to find that his teacher not only wasn't worried, he seemed actually to look forward to the hearing.

Mr. Kroeger had made arrangements for his students to attend the pre-trial hearing where the judge would listen to the charges brought by the police to see if there was enough evidence to warrant a real court trial. It was to be part of their journalism studies—a field trip. And he had alerted all the town's newspapers and radio and television stations that "journalism was being tested in the courtroom."

Mike was grateful that there was only a week until the pre-trial. He didn't think that his nerves could stand a long wait. He and Nita argued every time they saw each other about whether or not to tell Mr. Kroeger the truth. Each time, he let Nita convince him that the charges would be dismissed at the pre-trial.

"Look at Kroeger," she argued. "Don't you think he'd be worried if he thought he was headed for jail?"

Mike had to admit Nita was right about that. As the time grew nearer, Mr. Kroeger seemed to grow cheerier.

The day of the pre-trial, Mike stopped off at the courthouse cafeteria. Scanning the booths, he saw two men and a woman. Several cameras were on the table between them.

"Are you reporters?" he asked the woman nearest the aisle.

"I am," she replied. "Belle Friche from the *Telegram.*"

Mike introduced himself. "I'm wondering about that Judge Benderthorp. Any chance he'll be easy on Kroeger?"

The woman rolled her eyes slightly. "Who doesn't wonder about Benderthorp! He's as tough as a junkyard dog, and he hates the press with a passion."

Mike groaned. "That's what I was afraid of. Why?"

One of the men slid over and motioned for him to join them.

"He says we are biased," the woman answered. "He says our stories are more sympathetic to the criminal than to the victim."

Mike nodded. "I've heard that complaint before. Sometimes it's justified, don't you think?"

She shrugged. "Sometimes. We don't always follow

up on what happens to victims. Sometimes that's sloppy journalism, I suppose. But sometimes it's better to leave the victims alone so they can get their lives back to normal."

"Is that all that's bugging Benderthorp?" Mike asked.

"No," one of the photographers interrupted. "What really bugs him is his own kid was a junkie. The boy eventually died from an overdose. Judge Benderthorp blames us for dope dealers being out on the street. He says if we'd share our information, the cops could nail 'em. Guess thinking that's a lot easier for the judge than facing the real problems—like what made his kid take up drugs in the first place. Judge Benderthorp's as mean as the dickens to the press and to anybody he thinks is soft on dope."

Mike clicked his tongue against his teeth. It sounded like Mr. Kroeger was in for a really tough fight. Could he stand up to pressure from the judge? Mike wondered.

Mike walked with the reporter and photographers to the courtroom where Judge Benderthorp presided. The hearing was already underway, and Mr. Kroeger was on the stand. Mike spotted Nita near the back of the room. She'd saved him a seat.

He slid next to her and watched as the reporter and

photographers quietly made their way to a marked section. The judge seemed to glare holes through them as they took their places. He turned to Mr. Kroeger.

"You have no counsel?" the judge asked.

"No sir," he replied. "I didn't think I needed one."

Judge Benderthorp leaned forward. "You need a lawyer, sir. You need one. If you can't afford counsel the court will appoint one."

He nodded to the district attorney's representative, who turned to Mr. Kroeger.

"Do you understand that you are interfering with an ongoing investigation by refusing to divulge information you possess?" Attorney Johnson asked.

Mr. Kroeger replied, "No sir."

"No, you don't understand? Or no, you don't have the information?" Attorney Johnson asked.

"I mean no, I don't understand how I'm interfering with an ongoing investigation, sir," Mr. Kroeger replied.

"You do know the names of the student reporters who have the information we seek?"

"Yes sir, I do," Mr. Kroeger said.

Mike felt Nita's fingers dig into his hand. He reached to cover her hand with his, holding his breath.

"Will you give us the names of those student reporters?" the attorney asked.

Mr. Kroeger paused. He looked at the judge and the attorney, then out over the audience of his students.

"I cannot and will not reveal their names. I respectfully stand on the right of confidentiality."

Mike swallowed hard.

The judge rapped his gavel. "Do you realize you may be held in contempt of court if you refuse to answer?"

"If I tell you the names of the reporters here and now, I will begin an erosion of the freedom of the press." His voice grew louder. "Future journalists could be forced into revealing sources that are available to the police — with a little legwork of their own."

Mr. Kroeger paused a moment. "If we find out information, they can, too. And think of scandals and crimes that would never have been brought to the public's attention if people had been afraid to give reporters important information. People won't tell the press anything if they think their names will be made public. If we can no longer promise confidentiality, there will be no sources left — no one to tell on the powerful, no one — "

The judge gaveled his desk. "We asked for an answer, Mr. Kroeger, not a lecture on the *privilege* of the press to withhold information."

Mr. Kroeger nodded. He straightened up and

looked straight at the section where his students sat. "I do not believe it is the *privilege* of the press to withhold information, sir, but the *right*. My answer, sir, is that I refuse to answer. I will not submit my student reporters to pressure and danger. I stand on the right of the press to withhold information, even if my refusal means going to jail."

Mike let his breath out slowly.

The judge banged the gavel again. "Whether or not withholding information by the press is a right or a privilege will no doubt be debated in the higher courts for years to come. And those decisions—whatever they may be—will be challenged and appealed by both sides. You members of the press have been quick enough to insist on using information from government files for newspaper reporting. You say the public has a right to know. Does not the public have a right to know about criminals, too? Shouldn't all available information be used to get, and keep, criminals off the streets so they can't corrupt our children?"

The judge's voice choked momentarily, and Mike swallowed hard, remembering that the judge had lost his own son to drugs.

"Mr. Kroeger," Judge Benderthorp continued after a long pause, "your sincerity in what you consider the ethics of your profession—although I remind you that you are a teacher, and not a reporter—is admirable. Some judges might decide you are in the right. But it is the opinion of THIS court that your silence is not legally supportable.

"You have twenty-four hours to consult with your attorney and to consider the court's request. If after that time you still refuse to provide the information we seek, you will be held in contempt of court. You will be placed in the city jail until such time as you see fit to cooperate."

Mr. Kroeger's face looked strained. He rubbed his stomach gingerly. "Indefinitely, your honor? I can be held indefinitely?"

"You will be brought before this court each day, Mr. Kroeger. And each time you refuse to answer you will be guilty of a fresh case of contempt of court, punishable by imprisonment." He slammed his gavel. "There will be a fifteen minute recess. When the court reconvenes it will hear the case of the *People v. Gregory.*"

Mike didn't get up. He sat staring at Mr. Kroeger. His teacher remained sitting on the witness stand, smiling. A couple of photographers snapped pictures of him as his students clamored around.

"Can they do that?" Nita asked Mike. "I mean, there's really no time limit?"

Mike shrugged off Nita's questions. "Look at Kroeger!" he said in amazement. "He's never enjoyed himself so much."

"But he won't want to spend much time in jail—not without cameras and reporters and his admiring students gathered around him," Nita said.

She shrugged lightly. "It's just a bluff, Mike. Benderthorp will never jail Mr. Kroeger, believe me!"

Mike watched the judge as the crowd dispersed. Benderthorp didn't seem like one to reconsider his decisions.

"We've got to tell Mr. Kroeger about what we did," Mike said. "He'll understand, won't he?"

"We can't now," Nita said. "Things have gotten out of hand."

Mike knew Nita was right. Things had gotten out of hand. No matter which way they turned, they faced trouble. If they told the truth, Mr. Kroeger was going to lose his job for sure, especially after all this publicity. He'd look like a fool, protecting them all this time when the story was a hoax. What other school district would hire him? What newspaper would trust Mr. Kroeger as a reporter?

Roland would be furious! The students would lose their newspaper. The school would probably never get a newspaper again, and all the kids would put the blame squarely where it belonged—on him and Nita. They'd be outcasts!

And what newspaper would ever trust him? Mike thought bitterly. He'd never get a job, even if by some miracle he did get a scholarship.

What a disappointment he'd be to his parents, Mike knew. "I have three sons—a doctor, a lawyer, and a liar," he could hear his mother saying.

If he and Nita continued to keep quiet, would the whole problem just disappear? Was Nita right?

Mike frowned. He was beginning to think that the only way to get out of trouble was to go through it, not around it.

CHAPTER ELEVEN

Mike fought his bed covers all night. Like everything else in his life, they were smothering him. He couldn't think straight anymore. Or maybe it was just that for the first time in his life he was thinking straight.

All the answers seemed so simple on the face of it. Go to Kroeger and tell him the truth. Go to the judge and tell him everything. Face the principal and his parents with the truth. Take whatever punishment they had to dole out, even if it meant failing the whole year. So he'd delay college a year—assuming any college would want him. At least he'd be clear of lies.

If it weren't for Nita, who kept saying they should keep quiet! He threw his pillow across the room. How could he tell the truth without getting her permission? They were in this mess together. Maybe he'd have to get that kooky blonde out of his life if he was ever going to straighten out his problems. He'd tell her . . . he'd tell her . . . He didn't know what he'd tell her.

He drifted into a fitful sleep at last.

The next day during his morning classes, Mike was

again trying to convince himself that nothing was going to happen to Kroeger, that no one was going to jail his teacher because of a prank gone awry.

But during journalism class two uniformed officers came to the J-room. The twenty-four hours the judge had given Mr. Kroeger were up. Mr. Kroeger had obviously realized the judge wasn't bluffing because he had a small overnight bag sitting by his desk.

He greeted the officers cordially. "Give your names to my reporters," he instructed. "Send the police a copy of the paper," he told the editor.

The officers handcuffed Mr. Kroeger.

"Do you have to do that, for crying out loud?" Mike asked. "You think maybe he's going to make a desperate break for it or something?"

"Now don't get uptight, son," one of the officers said. "It's just routine."

"I'm all right," Mr. Kroeger assured Mike with a wink. "Just be sure the daily papers and the stations all know I'm in jail."

"Yes sir," Nita said. "I'll tell the city editors to get photographers down to the city jail as soon as possible. I'm sure you'll get good coverage."

"Fine, fine," he said. "When you make a worthwhile statement about social justice, you want to make sure that everyone knows about it."

The principal's secretary, looking flushed and embarrassed, came in. "I'll stay here for the rest of the classes today," she told the students. "Tomorrow you'll have a regular substitute—" She glanced at Mr. Kroeger. "—that is, if we need one."

Mike and the other class members crowded together at the window and watched as the two officers led Mr. Kroeger to the blue and while police car parked at the curb out front. Cat calls and jeers floated from the line of open windows. It was hard to tell whether the students were yelling at the cops or cheering because a teacher—particularly the journalism teacher—was being taken away. Mike didn't figure that any of the kids outside the journalism class were rooting for Mr. Kroeger. Not even the stinking school system would help Kroeger! The principal had told him he was on his own, and the outcome would affect the renewal of his contract. Roland was probably hoping that Kroeger would fall on his face.

The squad car drove away.

Mike felt fury welling inside him—fury with the judge who'd ordered Mr. Kroeger jailed, fury with the school system for not backing Mr. Kroeger, fury with Nita and her wild, stupid imagination. But most of all he was furious at himself for ever having gotten into such an awful situation.

The whole thing had gone far enough. He made his decision. He had to tell Kroeger, no matter what Nita thought. If she was involved, well tough!

But he wouldn't tell anyone else, at least not now, not without Mr. Kroeger's permission. If people knew that drug exposé was phony, the journalism teacher would be in even greater trouble. Kroeger really cared about journalism. It wouldn't be fair if he lost respect — or worse — his job because of what Mike and Nita had done.

Mike made another decision. He'd try to get other people to understand Mr. Kroeger's point of view, to be on his side.

He whirled to face the editor. "Clint, I'd like to be the one to write a feature on Mr. Kroeger — a side feature to go with the main story on this thing."

"Great," Clint replied. "I'm personally going to do the editorial about freedom of the press and all that. Kroeger's arrest is the dumbest thing I ever heard of!"

"I'd like to do something, too," Nita said. "Maybe I could help Mike, huh?"

"No!" Mike snapped. "This is all mine, Nita. You've helped me enough." He spat the words out, regretting his sharpness when he saw Nita recoil in shock.

"Look," he said, softly. "Go with me to the jail, okay? Maybe we can get in to interview him. And I'll call some of his old newspaper buddies. I think Dad'll let me use the WATS line at his office."

Nita nodded, but the look of hurt was still there in her eyes.

With a lot of extra pleading, Mike managed to get himself and Nita permission to visit Mr. Kroeger in jail. Mike explained to the police that he was writing up the story for the school paper. He wondered if his story was convincing, or if Judge Benderthorp had given permission, figuring that Kroeger's students might influence the teacher to give in.

On the elevator up to the fourth floor of the police station, Mike cautioned Nita. "I've had enough of your ideas. Look where they've gotten us! And look where they've gotten Kroeger! So if you can't tell the truth, just be quiet in there and let me do the talking."

Nita looked as if she might cry any second, but she nodded agreement. He hated making her feel bad—she looked like a little girl who'd broken her best toy—but he felt better, just knowing he was doing what was right, at last.

They waited in a small room. It was divided by a counter topped by chicken-mesh wire. Straight chairs were on each side.

The walls were a smudged pea green and the room smelled of pine air freshener. "I don't believe this!" Nita grumbled. "You'd think Mr. Kroeger had robbed a bank or something. This is a disgusting place!"

"Cool it," Mike warned her. "We're here only as a special favor. Don't say something crazy and blow it for us, okay?"

Nita nodded, and the two of them sat down to wait. Shortly a green door opened and a man in uniform led Mr. Kroeger into the other side of the "cage."

The journalism teacher was smiling!

"A nice surprise!" he said. "My top reporters right on the job, huh? Did the afternoon papers run pictures?"

Mike frowned. He was driving himself crazy with guilt and here was Kroeger, having the time of his life!

"Glad to see you're enjoying yourself so much," Mike said bitterly. He glanced at the guard, who stood a few feet away. Then Mike leaned closer, whispering. "Mr. Kroeger, you can't stay here. Tell them our names, or we will."

"I certainly will not!" Mr. Kroeger grumbled. "And neither will you."

Mike stared at his hands a minute, not surprised to see them tremble. He looked back at Nita.

She shrugged. She'd still rather not tell Kroeger the truth, Mike knew. But she seemed to be saying that whatever Mike did would be okay.

"We made the story up," Mike said. "Do you understand? We just made the whole thing up to keep from getting into trouble. We cut class and we needed an excuse. That's a plain fact."

Mr. Kroeger's jaw slacked. His eyes narrowed into slits. "I don't believe you. You can't—"

Mike glared at Nita. If she didn't support his story, if she didn't tell the truth for a change—

"It's true," Nita said. "We—that is I—it was my idea. I'm sorry."

Mr. Kroeger's pudgy fingers tapped the wire mesh. "But what about that kid in the hospital? The one that fit your story description?"

"Just coincidence," Mike admitted. "I made up the guy in the story, but the guy who was beaten fit my description so closely that someone may have thought he was the one I wrote about. Or maybe his beating was coincidental. I just don't know."

"The messages in the lockers were real enough," Mr. Kroeger argued. "Someone is angry that we are covering a story on drugs."

"But we're telling the truth. We made up everything. We—"

"Nonsense," Mr. Kroeger said. "You are just trying to protect me. Do you honestly think that the judge will believe you made up the story? He'll figure you're just trying to get me out of jail. Anyway, all of what you say is beside the point now. Whatever you did, you hit on a raw nerve. You opened up something real.

"And aside from that, do you really think I'd go in and tell that judge this was a silly high school prank, a hoax? No. There's more at stake here than keeping you two in school. I'm fighting for a principle now—the right of the press to withhold sources. I'm protecting the whole system of journalism. You two jokers aren't going to stop me."

He leaned forward, speaking between his teeth. "You two just keep quiet. Do you understand?"

"No, I don't," Nita said. "What have the lies we've told got to do with the whole system of journalism? Why should we stand up for a story that's not true?"

Mr. Kroeger glanced back at the guard. "We're not talking about the truth now. The issue was—and is—whether or not a publisher can be forced to reveal a source. I could tell the judge your names. Then you and I could tell him the story was a hoax, a lie. But what would we gain? Your consciences would be cleared. I would get out of jail. But we would lose the chance to make legal history. No sir—I won't trade that off. This is my chance—my chance to do something important. Both of you just keep quiet."

He nodded goodbye and stood up with a scrape of

his chair. The guard opened the door, and the two of them disappeared.

Mike sighed. "I feel like Clark Kent just removed his glasses and there's nothing there but Clark Kent—no Superman. Do you believe Kroeger? I feel like I'm seeing him for the first time."

"Me, too," Nita said. "Do you think he really believes he's doing this for journalism? Isn't telling the truth the most important thing a journalist does?"

"I think he's on an ego trip. I'm not even sure he wants to believe us. He's right that we've opened something up—a hornet's nest, I think. At any rate, we've done all we can. We've told him the truth. If he chooses to ignore it, that's his problem, not ours. I'm not going to tell the judge and get Kroeger in trouble."

They waited for the elevator that would take them to the first floor lobby. When the doors swooshed open, Mike and Nita stepped inside. Mike glanced casually at the young man already on the elevator. He looked vaguely familiar.

Mike squinted at him. There were fading bruises around the man's eyes and stitches around his lip. Mike stared at the sandy hair, then at the ID badge on the young man's shirt pocket.

"Holy cow!" Mike yelled. "You—you're not a student at all. You're a cop!"

CHAPTER TWELVE

The young man paled and stepped back. Frowning, he took Mike's arm. "Come with me," he said.

"Mike," Nita asked, "what's going on? Who is he?"

Mike couldn't take his eyes off the young man's bruised and scarred face. "It's the phony student who was beaten up."

To the man, Mike said, "Am I under arrest? Where are we going?"

"Please—Mike, is it? When the elevator stops, just come with me and we'll find a place to talk. I'll answer your questions—as many as I can—and maybe you'll answer a few of mine. Okay?"

He released his grip on Mike's arm as the elevator stopped on the first floor. "The cafeteria is to our right. Let's get something to drink, okay? My treat."

They settled into a booth and ordered soft drinks. The young man sipped his cola silently a few minutes without looking at Mike or Nita. They glanced nervously at each other, waiting.

82

Finally Mike broke the silence. "It must hurt something awful to drink with your lip in stitches like that. I didn't expect to see you out of the hospital so soon." He laughed slightly. "I didn't expect to see you *here,* certainly."

"Believe me, I didn't expect to see *you* here, either, Mike, and—?" He paused.

"Nita," she replied hesitantly.

"Your name tag says you're Detective Richard Murphy," Mike said. "So you are obviously not Jerry Cranford, high school senior."

"We'd guessed as much already," Nita said. "You have no records, your home address is a phony, and nobody at your old school ever heard of you."

The young detective sighed and leaned back, shoving his drink toward the center of the table. "You kids really know how to dig for facts, I'll hand you that. You'll make good reporters one of these days—once you get it straight about what NOT to print.

"I wish I'd contacted you before you wrote the story. Maybe I could've explained how important it was for me to remain out of the limelight. Maybe—I should've covered my tracks better."

He shrugged. "That story in your school paper made me useless in the sting operation. I still don't know how you tagged me—it was you, wasn't it? When did you see me? It'd help me to know where I goofed, just in case I ever go undercover again."

Mike bit his lip. "You didn't goof. It was coincidence—a silly, stupid coincidence. I mean, neither of us saw you or saw anything. I just thought that stand of bushes would be a good spot for a drug drop. I used it as a scene for a hypothetical case."

Detective Murphy stared at Mike, his chin slack in obvious surprise. "You mean, you just got all that out of your head? What about the clothes? The physical description?"

Mike shrugged slightly. "Coincidence," he admitted. "Lots of kids wear those surplus jackets, and sandy blonde hair is pretty ordinary, too. We wrote the story because we cut class and needed an excuse. Then things got sort of out of hand. That's all—honest. Except that Mr. Kroeger didn't know anything about this until today. We just told him."

The young man across from them squeezed his eyes shut. His shoulders heaved in a silent laugh. "I don't believe it! I spend four months establishing myself as a student in that school—going through classes I'd already taken, trying to get myself accepted into the drug operation. Four months of cheering the football team, listening to teachers tell me what I already knew, carrying girls' books to class—for what? The whole lousy

84

operation down the tubes because of an overactive imagination and — "

"I'm sorry," Mike said. It seemed he had done a lot of apologizing lately. But what else could he do?

"Sorry! You're sorry?" Detective Murphy snapped. "It'll take the rest of the year just to place another undercover cop in your school — if there's anyone on the force that looks young enough, that is. Sorry! You know how many kids could get hooked in that time? How many of them could commit crimes — maybe violent ones — to get the money for their drugs? That some of them might just get killed in the process, or from overdoses?" He touched his bandage. "You know, the people who beat me up could have killed me! I willingly put my life on the line to keep dope out of the hands of kids. But I don't expect the people I work for — the citizens — to be my enemies, too."

Even as Detective Murphy talked, an idea churned in Mike's head. A terrific idea. He could feel the plan bubbling to the top of his mind with such clarity he didn't doubt for a minute that it'd work. He knew he had to make amends — to journalism, to this young cop, maybe even to Kroeger and himself, even if he and his teacher didn't particularly deserve it. He leaned forward and let the words tumble from his mouth.

"Use me as an undercover man! I'm already at school. I'm a student and everyone knows me. I don't have to get established. Who'd suspect me? Please — it's the least I can do."

The young man glanced around the cafeteria, then leaned across the table. Mike could smell the adhesive of his bandages.

Detective Murphy spoke through clenched teeth. "You have got to be out of our mind. Look at me! I'm supposed to be a warning to others. I'm an example of the drug operation's handiwork. You want this to happen to you? Or worse?"

"Mike, please," Nita said, covering his hand with her own. "He's right. He's trained for this. You're — we're not. Undercover work's dangerous."

Mike shook his head vigorously. "If you don't help me, Detective Murphy, I'll go ahead on my own. Don't you see? I've made up my own mind without anybody planting the suggestion. With or without your guidance I'm going to track down the people in the school drug operation. But I think my chances are better with your help."

The young detective eyed Mike and Nita cautiously. "Do you have student IDs?"

Mike and Nita pulled out their identification cards and handed them to Detective Murphy. He wrote down their names, phone numbers, and addresses. Mike winced, imagining how difficult it was to hold a pencil in those swollen, bruised fingers.

Detective Murphy handed the IDs back, pausing to study Mike's and Nita's faces.

Then he buried his face in his hands, as if thinking about Mike's offer. Finally he sighed a surrender. "I can't stop you from looking around, keeping your eyes open, of course. All I can do is advise you *not* to go undercover. But if you insist, I can offer my assistance —unofficially, of course. I'm on sick leave for a week. I just came to the station to clear up some paper work."

He sighed again. "At least let me in on what you're doing, where you'll be, okay? Check with me once a day—right after school—whether or not you find out anything. And be sure to call me if you come up with any leads. Don't follow through on any leads yourself, all right?"

Mike nodded and extended his hand. Detective Murphy shook it.

"What should we do about Kroeger?" Mike asked. "Can you do anything to get him out of jail?"

"His face has been in every paper, along with his statements about knowing the identities of the reporters who witnessed the drug exchange. He's safer in jail where they can keep an eye on him, especially since he's in a cell by himself. Besides, from what I hear, he's having a ball.

"Be careful," he warned, sliding from the booth. He

pulled a piece of paper from his pocket and wrote a number on it. "This is my telephone at home. And this is my extension here at the station. If anything — anything at all — turns up, you call me at home. If I'm not there, call my extension here. They'll know how to get in touch with me. No heroics. Understand? Call me."

He strode from the cafeteria, leaving Mike and Nita to finish their drinks in silence.

"Well," Mike said, shoving his empty glass to the center of the table. "I guess I've got my work cut out for me."

Nita touched his hand. "Wrong," she corrected. "*We've* got *our* work cut out for *us*."

CHAPTER THIRTEEN

"Nita," Mike said as they descended the steps of the police station, "I wish you'd reconsider helping me."

"Why?" Nita asked. "Are you reconsidering?"

"No, of course not!" he replied. "But the work could be dangerous."

"And I'm a girl? Well, forget that excuse," Nita snapped. "Remember, I started all this in the first place. I HAVE to help. I want to feel better about what's happened as much as you do."

Mike took Nita's hand. "Listen, one of my favorite tricks has been blaming you everytime I get into trouble. But the truth is, I have choices. I don't have to go along with your wacky ideas—any of them."

Mike felt better, just saying that. He felt as if he'd grown up some. He'd made a start, anyway.

Nita grinned at him, appreciation in her eyes. "Thanks, Mike. But that goes double. I have choices, too. And I haven't always made the best ones."

They boarded the bus back to their neighborhood. Nita got off two stops earlier than Mike. As she rose to leave, he grabbed her hand. "Maybe tonight we can each make a list of places close to the school that would make good drug distribution points."

"Okay," Nita said. She bent to kiss him lightly on the cheek. "Bye."

The bus jerked away from the stop. Mike touched his cheek where Nita had kissed him. Catching sight of his own reflection in the bus window, he noticed he was grinning at nothing. Or was it nothing?

After all, he'd taken some big strides today. He'd told the truth—finally. He'd tried to square with Kroeger, although his confession had seemed to fall on deaf ears. He had begun to straighten out his relationship with Nita. And maybe with some careful snooping he could even square things with Detective Murphy.

When Mike got home, his father was dishing out beef stew from the crock pot. The strong smell of tomato made Mike realize he was famished. It was the first time he'd felt really hungry in a long time.

"Hi," he greeted his father. "Mom working late?"

"Yes, they're bidding a new project in the morning and all of them are working late to get the bid ready. It's a biggie, she says."

"That's great. Hope they get it," Mike said sincerely.

Mike's father set their two plates on the yellow Formica table. Mike pulled the forks and spoons from the drawer. He set out glasses of milk—somehow milk seemed to taste its best with stew.

"You've been to see your journalism teacher —what's his name?" his father asked.

"Kroeger," Mike replied. "Yes sir, Nita and I went to see him. I think he's actually enjoying his stay in jail. Maybe he likes getting away from us kids, huh?" he said lightly. He hoped his father would drop the subject.

He didn't. "I wish him luck! I hear that Judge Benderthorp is the toughest to deal with in our judicial system. He's not all that fond of newspapers, either."

"Well, gosh, Dad," Mike said. "It's only a high school paper. What's he getting so uptight about?"

His father sipped some milk, then replied thoughtfully, "I guess he doesn't want to do anything that might be used as a precedent in other cases. I have to admire Kroeger. He must really believe in what he's doing. But it does look like those reporters could come forward and turn themselves in."

"But maybe they don't want to make a fool out of Kroeger. Maybe the whole thing is a lot more com-plicated than it appears."

"Complicated? What's more complicated than kids getting into drugs? I thank my lucky stars that my three sons have shown some sense, what with all the bad in-fluences there are today. I don't know—maybe Judge

Benderthorp is right. Maybe the law should force reporters to reveal their sources in drug cases. Anything to get the pushers off the streets!"

"But, Dad!" Mike argued. "You can't decide this kind of law on a case by case basis. You can't say reporters have to reveal sources in drug cases but can keep quiet if they're dealing with white collar crime. The law has to be consistent."

He got up to get himself some more stew. "Remember the story about the vice president of your company—the one who was stealing funds? Do you think the reporter who wrote it would have ever gotten the information he needed if he hadn't promised some guy his name would be kept secret? And what would have happened if that story hadn't been written? Your company might have gone bankrupt. The vice president was even dipping into the pension fund! He would have been living like a king while everyone else was out of work."

"Ummm, well," Mr. Bradshaw said, dabbing his mouth. "I guess it's not a simple issue." He carried his plate to the sink. "We don't need to keep the stew hot. Your mother is eating with the office staff."

He turned to Mike. "Homework?"

"I, er, have some stuff I have to do," Mike said. "Oh, Dad! Can I use your WATS line tomorrow? I need to make a long distance call for a story that's due."

"Sure," his father said. "Come to my office after school and then I'll give you a ride home."

Mike excused himself and went to his room. He pulled out a notebook and pencil and flopped across his bed to think. Across the top left side of the paper he wrote, "Places Close to School Where Kids Hang Out." On the right he wrote, "Activities and Opportunities."

He started his list:

"Pop's Place—always crowded with kids. Drug activities could go unnoticed in crowds."

That was easy, but what other drug distribution places were there? he wondered. He closed his eyes, picturing the businesses that bordered the school.

"The grocery store—delivery trucks go in and out unnoticed. A few kids work there as stockers and baggers. Maybe drugs could be brought in without attracting too much attention.

"The service station—only two people work there, a man and his son, I think. It might be a place to distribute drugs. There are soft drink and candy machines and kids hang around a lot."

He remembered a laundromat, with only one employee who worked there all the time, making change and selling portions of soap and bleach. Kids went there for soft drinks sometimes. "Maybe the attendant dispenses more than soap?" he wrote.

Mike stared at his list. He had written down four places. He couldn't watch them all, he knew. Which ones were the most suspicious? He was impatient to get started. He pulled the phone into his room and dialed Detective Murphy's phone number.

"Rick Murphy," a voice answered.

"Detective Murphy? This is Mike—you know, the guy you met a while ago at the er—the station."

"Yeah. What's up, Mike?"

"I made up a list of places close to the school and I wanted to test your reaction—see which ones you think I ought to stake out."

There was a muffled cough on the other end of the line. Mike wished he hadn't said "stake out." That cop must think I'm a real gung-ho jerk! he thought.

"Okay, Mike, I'm listening," the police officer said.

"The laundromat."

"The attendant is a sixty-year-old grandmother," Detective Murphy said. "Of course, that doesn't make her immune from crime, but it puts her and her laundromat way down the list of possibilities, I'd say."

"Right," Mike admitted, feeling a little silly. "Pop's," he continued.

"Yeah, it's possible drugs are distributed there. But I've hung around the place until I knew every price by heart and never turned up anything even mildly suspicious. I'd keep my eyes open, if I were you, but I wouldn't go in with guns blazing."

Mike took a deep breath. "The service station?"

"It's possible. I haven't had the chance to check it out yet. The station's run by a man and his son."

"The grocery store?" Mike said.

"Again, possible. So far, nothing's turned up. But that doesn't mean something won't. That all?"

"Yeah," Mike admitted. "Except for the church and the florist, but I didn't even write those down. Kids don't hang out at either of those places."

"A good detective doesn't dismiss things because they look okay on the surface," Officer Murphy said.

Mike wondered if Murphy was humoring him. But he was determined to prove to the young cop that he could be a good detective.

"I'll keep you posted on anything I find," Mike said.

There was a stifled sigh on the other end. "Okay, Mike. Keep me posted." The line clicked dead.

Rick Murphy *was* just humoring him.

Mike regretted calling the young detective with no real information. He promised himself he'd not make that mistake again.

CHAPTER FOURTEEN

The next day at lunch Mike and Nita compared notes.

"I can't dismiss the florist as easily as you," Nita told Mike. "After all, he gets deliveries all the time in those little closed-in trucks. The drivers pull right up to the back door." Nita grinned. "And plants are *potted*."

"Ouch, that really hurts!" Mike laughed in spite of himself. "Thanks for the corny joke, Nita. I needed it. I think I'm getting too wrapped up in this thing. I can't get it out of my head that with one silly story I've gotten a classroom and car vandalized, my teacher arrested, a guy beaten up, and a whole police undercover investigation blown."

Nita patted his arm. "I know. I don't feel any better than you do. If I hadn't conned you into writing a phony story, none of these things would've ever happened."

Mike reached to tousle her bangs. "Listen, I'm telling you again, if there's one thing I've learned about myself in these midnight soul-searchings, it's that I don't have to do what I don't want to. It's my choice—to botch up my life or to do the right thing."

Nita squeezed his hand. "Thanks."

"But what about the other possibilities on my list? Murphy pretty well dismissed the laundromat. He said an old lady runs it. But he hadn't checked the service station or the grocery store. I have the feeling that he thinks we're just kids noodling around in grown-up work. I'd like to show him."

"Yeah," Nita agreed. "I have the feeling that we're missing something—something that is so obvious that we just can't see it. Something that is a part of the scenery—like the graffiti in the hall."

"But what—or who—are we overlooking?" Mike wondered aloud. "Grown-ups that work around the school, maybe? The janitors? The cooks or serving people in the cafeteria? "

"Maybe," Nita said, "but don't the health inspectors come unannounced to check out the kitchen? A drug dealer wouldn't be able to take a chance that an inspector would uncover something."

"Yeah, you're right," Mike agreed.

The melodic sound of a calliope drew closer. An ice-cream wagon pulled away from the florist shop and stopped in front of Mike and Nita. Mike glanced at his watch. "The ice-cream man—right on time. You want a cone before we go back in?" he asked Nita.

They strolled toward the curb and joined a scattering of other students. A young man in a white smock hopped from the cab of the ice-cream wagon and grinned at them. "Yeah? Wha'd'ya need today?"

"An eskimo pie," Nita said.

"A drumstick," Mike answered.

Another girl joined them. "Whoops!" she said as she momentarily lost her balance and stumbled against Mike. She slurred an apology, then giggled as Mike steadied her.

Mike paid for his and Nita's ice cream and took Nita's arm, leading her from the group.

He glanced back at the girl. "She was spaced out of her mind. Did you see her eyes? She didn't look like she knew whether she was standing or sitting."

He slapped his forehead. "Are you thinking what I'm thinking? I mean, how can we have such tunnel vision? We're looking for someone in daily contact with the students. What about—" He waved a hand toward the ice-cream wagon.

"The thought gives me the creeps," Nita said. "I mean, ice cream is so—so innocent! And little kids hang around the wagon. Oh, Mike, I hope you're wrong."

"I hope so, too. But I think we should definitely put it on our list of places to watch, don't you?"

He stood nibbling his drumstick, watching while the remaining students hovered around the ice-cream truck. The girl that had stumbled against Mike was among the last to be served. She and the driver walked around to the other side of the truck. She returned with an ice-cream sandwich, still walking unsteadily.

"My gosh!" Nita said. "Do you see her? She's sticking that ice cream in her purse! By next period she'll have a purse full of goop!"

"I think she's stoned," Mike admitted. "It'd be funny if it wasn't so sad."

That afternoon there was a substitute teacher in journalism class. Seeing a stranger in front of the room reminded Mike that he had promised the editor he'd write a feature article on Mr. Kroeger. After what had happened at the jail, Mike didn't feel the same about his teacher. But he had promised to do the story.

He went to his father's office after school.

"Use the phone on my desk," his father told him. "You know the system, don't you?"

Mike nodded, pleased that his father trusted him so much he didn't even ask who or where he was calling. He vowed to become worthy of that trust. Mike pulled a phone number from his billfold and dialed.

When the switchboard answered he said, "City editor, please." He tried to deepen his voice just a little. "This is Mike Bradshaw with the *Campus Caller*." He decided not to mention that he worked for a high school paper. "I'm looking for some background information on a former reporter of yours, Rob Kroeger."

"Kroeger...Kroeger..." the man said. "I don't recollect a Kroeger—Rob you say? I've been here only ten years—maybe he was before my time. Let me ask one of the old-timers to get on the line."

Mike heard the man call, "Mathis, line two. See if you can help this guy, will you?"

The phone made a hollow sound as another receiver was lifted. "Yeah? This is Sam Mathis, copy desk."

"Mike Bradshaw," Mike responded. "I'm trying to get information about a Rob Kroeger who used to work for you. We're doing a feature on him. The city editor didn't seem to know him, but Mr. Kroeger worked at your paper more recently than ten years ago—five or six at the most."

"Kroeger," Sam Mathis replied. "Sounds vaguely familiar. Let me think."

"He covered some of your bigger stories—the mayor's scandal, the industrial kickback, a series on political blackmail—" Mike reeled off a list he'd heard Mr. Kroeger talk about.

"Ummm, Mike, did you say? Mike, I was the one who did the stories on industrial kickback. And Dickerson did the mayor's scandal stories—even the research."

"Well, I know Mr. Kroeger wrote a feature that

helped clean up a dirty films racket," Mike persisted.

There was a long sigh. "Hang on a minute. Let me get on the line to personnel."

Mike tapped his pencil nervously while he waited. What was going on, anyway? How could they forget one of their top reporters?

"Mike?" the man said. "Look, Kroeger did work here, until six years ago. But he wasn't what you'd call a reporter—not exactly. He did the obituary news and pilot news, you know, ships coming and going. He had that job—let me check these notes—for four years. Ummm, that's interesting."

"What is?" Mike asked, still trying to comprehend what the man was telling him.

"Most guys have that job about six months at the most. You know, they use it as a holding spot until a real reporting position opens up. It's a nothing job."

He mumbled something away from the phone that Mike couldn't understand. A second receiver was lifted. It was the city editor again.

"I remember Kroeger now. Nice guy, but I don't think the kind to be a big-time reporter. Just didn't have the spunk it took to dig up the tough stuff—know what I mean? Why did you say you were writing this story?"

Mike felt empty, as if someone had taken a plug out

of him and everything he was had just spilled to the floor.

Kroeger was just a big phony. All those stories he'd told about his career were lies. He'd been a nothing at newspaper work. Why had he lied to his students? Why had he tried to make them believe he was someone important?

"It doesn't matter," he replied. "Thanks." He hung up just as his father returned.

"Finished?" his father asked. "I can take you home, if you'd like."

Mike nodded numbly and followed his father to the car. They drove in silence as Mike tried to sort through what he'd learned.

He spotted Nita's street. "Let me off here, Dad," Mike said. He didn't really understand what he'd found out, but he felt he needed to share it, even if it meant facing Rapunzel in her ivory tower.

He went in through the wrought iron gate and mounted the marble steps to the large, double, oak doors. He pushed the doorbell and heard chimes inside.

The door opened and an elderly woman in a maid's uniform answered.

"I'm Mike Bradshaw. May I see Nita?" Mike asked, feeling a little awed. He hadn't expected a maid to answer the door.

"Mike—of course! You're just as my granddaughter described you," the woman said. "But you have the wrong house, dear. We live in the servants' quarters."

Mike backed away, feeling the blood rush from his head. "Servants' quarters!" His mouth hung open. The servants' quarters? Nita's grandmother was the maid of this house, not the owner?

He spun around and darted for the gate.

"You're going the wrong way!" the woman called. "It's just back through the path! Follow the slate walk—"

The woman's words faded as he burst through the gate. Mike felt his ears burn. Nita'd lied to him. All these years she had made him think that her family was something special and he wasn't even fit to go into their house. Her grandmother wasn't strict, after all. Rapunzel had constructed her own ivory tower all along. She'd locked herself inside and hung up a no trespassing sign for him. She had *lied*.

Nita had lied.

Mr. Kroeger had lied.

Was no one to be trusted any more?

Mike swallowed hard. Could he honestly tell himself that he was any different? He felt bloated from the lies he knew—his own and everyone else's.

CHAPTER FIFTEEN

Mike sat staring at his supper. He wasn't hungry. He felt already full — full of lies.

"Mike, we're talking to you. Are you all right?" his mother asked.

"You haven't seemed the same since your long distance call," his father said. "Couldn't you get the information you needed? Can we help?"

"I guess nobody can help," Mike said. "It's something I have to sort through myself. But thanks, anyway." He excused himself and went upstairs to fling himself across the bed and try, once again, to sort things through.

For once his tiny bedroom seemed too big and empty. It had been so jammed when his brothers were home. He wished one of them was here now. Maybe he could — no, he reminded himself. He had to work through his own problems.

Mike couldn't decide which bothered him more, Nita or Mr. Kroeger. He'd known Nita practically all his life. She'd always had a wild imagination. She made up stories as easily as she told the truth—maybe even more easily. Maybe she'd built this myth about herself to impress other people and ended by believing it herself. But why had she tried to impress him? He was supposed to be her friend.

What about Mr. Kroeger? He was a grown-up, for crying out loud. Weren't grown-ups supposed to outgrow make-believe?

Mike had a good mind to write Mr. Kroeger's background up. That'd show him. Mr. Kroeger had helped to get him and Nita into trouble. If he hadn't egged them on, made them feel like big-time reporters, told them all his wild tales about—

"Stop that, Mike," he told himself. "There you go again. Nobody got you into trouble but you."

It was so easy to see how a lie grew. First it was just a little fib, then it got bigger and bigger until it became so huge it choked off your air. Finally, if you didn't do something about it, the lie became like the truth, and you had to live with it, no matter what.

He rolled over and stared at the ceiling, watching the darkening shadows. So Mr. Kroeger had been a nowhere reporter. He couldn't make it in big-time reporting the way he'd wanted to. Maybe he'd borrowed all those stories to impress his students or even to inspire them.

And now the lies were catching up with Kroeger. Mike had found him out. The faculty would just love to know what Mike knew. And some of the students would, too.

But what would be gained by disgracing Kroeger? Mike knew he couldn't tell everyone the journalism teacher was a phony. It was up to Mr. Kroeger. What right did Mike have to punish someone else for lying — he'd done so much of it himself!

And Nita? If she wanted to be a princess in a fairy tale was it his place to call her bluff? He didn't care where she lived. Yet could they be real friends if Nita felt she had to lie to him? Didn't real friends have to accept and trust each other?

Mike vowed he'd say nothing about either discovery — not ever.

It was the next day at lunch before he saw Nita again. He realized she'd probably been avoiding him, just as he had her. He flushed with his secrets.

Her eyes met his and he knew — her grandmother had told her.

"Mike, I — I've got to talk to you. I've got to explain something. I'm so sorry."

Mike breathed a sigh of relief. He touched his fingertips to her cheek. "Later," he said. "We have some other things to set straight — some other lives to

106

make amends to—before we clear up our own past. Okay?"

Right now, just knowing that Nita wanted to tell him everything was enough for him. He could see she was genuinely upset. They could work things out, later—he hoped.

"I think we should check the ice-cream wagon and everyplace else we can think of. Murphy missed the service station. I'll take my bike over there this afternoon," he said, changing the subject. "Maybe I can hang around long enough to see if the kids are getting any dope there."

"Sure," Nita agreed. "And I'll check on the grocery store, maybe flirt with the produce stocker," she said, obviously relieved to drop the subject of her lie.

Mike grinned. "He's an old guy, probably thirty."

"Then I'll just pretend to be doing comparison shopping for home economics or something. I'll keep my eyes open for anything suspicious," she said.

They heard calliope music as they talked. "Here comes the ice-cream man," Mike said. "Let's watch closely. If he's passing stuff, maybe we can spot it, okay? Just act naturally."

They chatted as they watched the white truck with its red sign come closer to the campus. It stopped in front of the florist, as it had the day before.

The driver slid from the truck with his portable pack slung over his shoulder and went inside.

"Either that florist is a worse ice-cream junkie than we are," Nita said, "or there's something going on between him and the ice-cream man. The florist doesn't even have to flag down the truck. The guy just automatically stops every day."

Mike nodded, watching for the man to emerge from the florist shop. "He's not a whole lot older than we are and he looks like he's making lots of money. Did you get a load of that ring he was wearing yesterday? And that watch! No Mickey Mouse or Kermit the Frog for him!"

Nita grinned. "In the ice-cream business you need plenty of 'ice.'"

"Poor joke, Nita!" Mike chided. "I can tell you're a writer. You have such a way with words!"

The ice-cream man came out of the florist shop. He stuffed some packages into the far side of his truck and got in.

The music tinkled as the truck moved forward and came to a halt at the school's main sidewalk. Mike and Nita joined the other kids and waited their turn to buy ice cream.

Mike glanced at the man's hand. There were at least ten karats worth of diamonds in his ring. His watch had diamonds instead of numbers. Of course, the diamonds on the ring and watch could be phony, but they sure looked real. Mike winked at Nita.

"Drumstick?" the man asked.

"Yeah," Mike said. "How'd you remember?"

"Great memory," the man replied, flashing a grin.

Mike looked at the little engraved name tag on the man's pocket. Sam Shavelle, it said.

Shavelle got Mike the drumstick and Nita an Eskimo pie and handed Mike his change. Then he went to the other side of the truck to serve some other kids, waving a friendly goodbye to Nita and Mike.

"He acts so nice," Nita said. "I hate to think he's mixed up in drugs. Still, it looks awfully suspicious, doesn't it? I mean the way he takes some kids to the other side of the truck — as if he doesn't want anyone to see what he gives them."

"And if those jewels are real, I don't think he could get them on ice-cream earnings, do you?" Mike added. "But if he is pushing drugs, he's not alone. He has to get his stuff from somewhere, like maybe that flower shop. Or maybe the service station — he makes a regular stop there. Come to think of it, I've seen the ice-cream truck at the grocer's, too."

"Well, we have to check out all those places," Nita said.

Mike sighed wearily. None of this was looking easy.

CHAPTER SIXTEEN

That afternoon Mike rode his bike to the corner nearest the service station, then stopped and let the air out of one of his tires. He pushed his bike into the station driveway.

"Hi!" the owner said, waving a grease-stained hand in Mike's direction. "Looks like you've got a square wheel. The air gauge is on top of the unleaded pump."

Mike nodded. He got the gauge and placed it against the valve. Then he pretended to stretch as he watched a crowd of students near the candy machines, joking with the man.

Mike put a little air in the back tire, too, then replaced the gauge.

"Are you new at school?" the man asked. "I don't remember seeing you around before."

"No sir, I'm not new," Mike replied. "I just usually go straight home, that's all."

"Good boy!" the man said. "My kid"—he nodded in

the direction of the younger man—"always came straight here from school and helped me out. Never had to worry about what he was up to—no sir. Not like with some kids these days."

Mike nodded agreement. "Thanks for the air," he called.

He rode on home. It was a waste of time, watching that guy and his son. They weren't the types to sell drugs—not at all.

Maybe Nita would have better luck at the grocery store.

They met after school the next day, and Mike discovered that Nita had found nothing unusual at the grocery store, either. "The manager got tired of my hanging around the magazine racks," Nita admitted. "He finally ran me off—said I was distracting his checkers." She fluffed her hair dramatically. "Imagine me, distracting!"

"I think our best bet is to just concentrate on the ice-cream guy," Mike said.

"Yeah, I think so, too," Nita admitted. "I watched him at noon today and he went through the same routine as before. He went into the florist and stayed a long time, then he came over to the school. He sold some of the kids ice cream from one side of the wagon and some from the other."

Mike snapped his fingers. "You remember the other day? That girl put her ice-cream sandwich into her purse. We thought it was funny, that it'd melt. But, do you think there might have been something other than ice cream inside the wrapper?"

"We need to get a better look at the operation, that's for sure," Nita said. "Maybe you could distract Shavelle tomorrow while I peek in the other side of the truck. What do you think?"

Mike laughed. "You do the distracting, remember?" He frowned, remembering. "You know, someone beat up Detective Murphy. And I don't think that person would hesitate to get us, either."

"Hey!" the editor of the school paper called to Mike. "I thought you were going to do a side feature on Mr. Kroeger. What's the hold up?"

Mike frowned. He'd hoped that Clint would forget all about the assignment. "Er, no. I—I haven't had time—"

"I can assign it to someone else."

"No—no, don't do that," Mike said. "I'll do it."

He didn't want anyone else to find out what he'd uncovered about Mr. Kroeger.

"Make it snappy, will you?"

"Life is so complicated!" Mike muttered to Nita when Clint had left. "I can't do that story on Kroeger because—never mind." He didn't even want to tell Nita.

"Do you think Sam Shavelle and the florist work together?" Nita asked.

"It's possible," Mike said. "I know the florist doesn't have a greenhouse. He doesn't grow any of his own flowers. All his stuff comes in from somewhere else by truck. Maybe flowers aren't all that comes in that way. Maybe the florist gets drugs and distributes them to little guys, like Shavelle. Maybe Shavelle is just a small wheel in a really big operation. If he's dealing with the schools and we can prove it, maybe he'd talk to the police about the rest of the operation."

"If you think the florist is involved, let's concentrate on him. Let's stake out those trucks that deliver flowers," Nita said.

Friday was a teacher in-service day and the students didn't have to attend classes. Mike and Nita rode their bikes to the school yard, locked them, then strolled casually across the street and slipped into the alleyway behind the florist.

"I brought snacks," Nita said. "Peanuts, celery, a couple of sandwiches, and a thermos of lemonade. I figured we might get hungry."

"Smart move," Mike said, wondering why he hadn't thought of anything but carrot sticks. "There's no telling how long before we spot anything—if we spot anything, that is."

They hid behind a stack of crates—close enough to see the florist's back door—and settled into cramped positions.

Mike glanced at his watch. "It's 8:30 now. What if the flowers have already been delivered? Or what if there's no delivery on Fridays?"

"Then we'll go home, I guess. And we'll leave this detective work to the police—which we probably should be doing anyway," Nita answered.

Mike shot her a quick glance. "If you don't want to go through with this, I'll understand."

Nita opened the peanuts and offered Mike some. "I didn't say that. We're in this together—all the way."

The next time Mike glanced at his watch it was 10:30. The only other living thing in the alley was a stray cat.

Mike felt as if his eyes were going to pop out, he'd stared so long.

Nita poked his arm and offered him a sandwich, which he accepted. What a drag, this waiting was!

The sun was straight up when Nita shifted, nearly toppling a crate.

"Sorry," she apologized. "My legs are cramped. Maybe we should go home. What do you think?"

"Shhh!" Mike hissed. He nodded toward the end of the alley.

A panel truck marked "Floral Warehouse" pulled into the alley. Nita and Mike watched two men unload potted plants. One man tapped on the back door of the florist's and someone opened the door. The men carried load after load of the plants inside.

One of the men stumbled as he stepped from the truck. He fell to the driveway, dropping his load. A plant spilled from its pot. Scattered across the alley were small packets of white powder.

Drugs were being smuggled into the florist's hidden in pots.

"Clean that up and get inside, quick, before someone sees you, stupid!" the other man barked. Quickly the two scooped up the white packets and stuck them back inside the pot, placing the plant on top of them.

"I can't believe it, but we were right!" Mike whispered, turning to Nita.

He was alone in the alley. "Nita?" he whispered hoarsely. "Where are you, Nita?"

The men who'd unloaded the truck paused at the door of the florist and called, "See you Monday."

Mike crouched lower behind the trash cans as the men turned back toward their truck. He dared not breathe, for fear they'd discover him.

One of the men slammed the panel door of the truck shut, then the two of them climbed into the cab. The motor rumbled to life.

"Nita?" Mike whispered. "Nita—where are you?"

The truck was beginning to pull away. Mike hastily brought out his note pad and wrote down the license plate number: XPO 999. He scribbled a quick description of the truck and the men.

His eyes flickered upward from the license plate to the small glass panel in the rear door of the truck. Mike felt his legs go limp under him.

It was clearly Nita's face in the window. She had stowed away on the truck!

He didn't dare stop to call Detective Murphy. He had to hurry. He couldn't let that truck out of his sight—not with Nita trapped inside. There was no telling what the men might do if they caught her.

As soon as the truck turned the corner, Mike jumped on his bike and sped after it—and Nita. The truck roared down the busy street and almost ran the first red light. It wasn't going to be easy to keep up.

But pictures flashed into his mind of Detective Murphy's beat-up face, and Mike pedaled with renewed vigor.

CHAPTER SEVENTEEN

Mike frantically pedaled to keep up with the van as it rounded the next corner.

Did the men know Nita was inside the truck? he wondered. Did they plan to take her far away from prying eyes and then get rid of her? He willed his legs to keep pushing. He leaned forward so his body would offer less resistance to the wind.

It seemed that the van traveled forever, stopping only a few times for red lights, allowing him to catch up a little. He pushed from his mind the possibility that the men might have seen him following. Could they be going slowly deliberately so that they could capture him as well as Nita?

Finally the van turned into a drive by a row of rental warehouses. Mike skidded to a halt and pulled his bike behind some parked trucks. He positioned himself so he had a good view of the back of the truck.

Maybe the men would just go inside one of the warehouses without ever seeing Nita. If they did, he could let her out of the truck and the two of them could call Murphy once she was safe. Mike's breath caught in his throat. The van door was open. They'd found her!

One of the guys pulled Nita, kicking furiously at his shins, from the van. The two men shoved her into one of the warehouses.

Mike's mind raced. Should he go bursting in there and try to get her loose, or should he call for help first? He'd better call for help, he decided. If he didn't, and he was caught, no one might ever know what had happened to him or Nita.

He remembered passing a phone booth at the front of the warehouse park. Fishing through his jeans as he ran, he found enough coins to make a call. He burst into the booth and plunged the money into the slot. He breathed a sigh of relief as he heard the dial tone, then felt his heart nearly stop as he remembered Murphy's number was home on his desk.

Numbers danced through his head, but none of them made any connection. He'd have to dial headquarters. But what was the switchboard number? There was no phone book in the booth.

He dialed "911," the police emergency number.

When the dispatcher answered, Mike asked for Detective Murphy.

"This is for emergency calls only. Call through the switchboard," the dispatcher instructed him.

"No!" Mike yelled. "Don't hang up!" He explained the situation in halting, frantic sentences.

"Help is on the way," the dispatcher said. "And I'll alert Detective Murphy."

When Mike hung up, he felt perspiration beading his lip and hairline. He'd promised the dispatcher not to do anything but wait. And he'd promised Murphy that he wouldn't try anything heroic. But he had to know that Nita was all right. If there was anything he could do to save her—

Blindly he stumbled back toward the warehouses. Which door had they gone in? He had watched them, but now all the doors looked alike. Then he spotted something. Nita's purse lay open and spilled near one entrance.

Gingerly Mike tested the door handle. To his surprise it gave, and he pushed himself through the door and straight into the broad shoulders of one of the truckers.

The man stood facing another, even bigger, who held Nita's arm at what must have been a painful angle.

"Mike!" she gasped. "What are you doing here?"

"Look," the big man holding Nita said. "We've got two of them."

Suddenly an idea hit Mike. If he could make it work

119

he could stall until the police got there. Maybe he could keep himself and Nita from being hurt.

"Have you told them yet?" Mike asked her, hoping his voice had settled down.

"Told them?" Nita asked. Tears clung to her lashes. She sniffled. "Told them what?"

Mike gave her a quick scowl. She straightened slightly, catching on that he had a plan.

"No, I haven't told them," she said. "They've been too busy picking on me to listen. Maybe you better tell them."

"Yeah," the second man said. "Let's hear what you teenies possibly could say to keep us from killing you."

Mike swallowed hard. He felt lightheaded. He was afraid he might pass out if he didn't sit down. "Why don't we make ourselves comfortable," he said boldly. "I like to sit while I'm dealing."

The big man laughed. "Dealing! What kind of dealing could a kid like you do?"

What kind, indeed, Mike wondered. Could he pull this off? If only the cops don't stop for red lights on the way—

"I'm not that much younger than Sam. And I don't think he's doing a very good job for you at Travis school," Mike said.

The big man loosened his grip on Nita's arm.

"What do you mean by that? Is Shavelle holding out on us?"

"I didn't say that, exactly," Mike said. "That's something you and Sam will have to work out. I'm just saying that he's missing a lot of the market, and he's letting another dealer move in on him. I'd like to take his territory. I can guarantee you a better profit."

The man glanced at his partner and then at Nita. "What's she got to do with this?"

"She's with me," Mike said. "She can get places I can't, if you know what I mean. Oh, I'm not asking for a big cut for the both of us—" He listened anxiously—did he hear a siren in the distance? "We could just split whatever percent you give Sam now."

The man scowled at him. Mike felt he wasn't showing enough greed to sound believable. "I think that we can make more for each of us than Sam is making for himself. And of course, if we prove to be as good as I believe we are, we'll ask for more—a partnership, maybe."

He obviously had said the right thing because the big man suddenly broke out into laughter.

"You're gutsy, kid. I like your style!"

Mike knew there was no way these guys would go for his act—they were only stringing him along. But that was all right. He just wanted to buy a little time.

"He may be gutsy, but he's still a punk kid," the second man said. "Besides, how'd he find out about us? I don't like it, Bill."

"Sam talks a lot, you know," Nita said, obviously feeling a little more comfortable now that the grip on her was released. "Big mouths don't make good partners."

"Well, one thing's for sure," the big man said. "I got to check out Shavelle. He's been sloppy. We got to figure out what to do with him. We can't have mouthy help."

"What'll we do with the teenies?" the second man asked.

Mike felt himself go limp. The sirens he'd heard had faded away. He was running out of small talk. He didn't think he could stall these creeps much longer.

What if he'd given the dispatcher the wrong address? What if the dispatcher thought he was just a prankster? What if the police never came at all?

CHAPTER EIGHTEEN

Mike and the big guy heard it at the same time—something or someone outside scraping against something metal.

"Hey! What was that?" the man yelled.

Mike knew he wouldn't have another opportunity. He dove for the big guy. In the same instant Nita picked up a tape dispenser from the desk and slammed it against the other man's head.

The door burst open, and uniformed men leaped through the front entrance of the warehouse.

Nita flung herself into Mike's arms as Detective Murphy and the others rounded up the two men.

"You okay?" Mike asked.

"I am now," Nita said. "You?"

Mike nodded numbly. "Thanks," he told Detective Murphy. "I wasn't sure you'd gotten the message. I wasn't sure *anybody* had gotten the message," he admitted.

Rick Murphy grinned. "I was downtown when the call came in. I was seeing what I could do about getting

Kroeger out of jail, considering the unusual circumstances."

Mike's hopes soared. "Did you?"

"Yeah, but it took some talking!"

"Judge Benderthorp was that tough, huh?" Nita asked.

"No," Rick said. "It was Kroeger who was tough. He was determined he was going to stay in jail until he'd made his point. It took some negotiating to convince him he should tell the judge the story was phony. I really ought to get on you kids, but I'm just too glad things turned out the way they did—you two safe and us with a roomful of incriminating evidence. I've got a feeling these guys will be singing like little birds to save their own scalps. We'll probably get all the information we need about the school vandalism, the drug ring— everything."

"But don't leave out the ice-cream man, Sam Shavelle," Mike said. "He's the one who made us suspicious enough to follow the flower truck."

"Will do," Rick promised. "You two get on home," he added. "You can come in Saturday and make your statements. And, er, I think Judge Benderthorp will want to see you both. I'll go along with you. I'll tell him what you've done for us. Maybe that'll help."

Nita hitched on the back of Mike's bike, and the

two of them rode back to the florist's to get her bike. When they got there, a team of detectives were already closing in on the florist.

Impulsively Nita squeezed Mike's hand. "Have I told you you're terrific?"

"Not lately," Mike said, pushing off on his bike. "And I think it's about time you did."

"You're terrific!" she yelled after him.

On Saturday they made their statements at the police station and listened while Detective Murphy praised and scolded them for their foolish but effective efforts. He stood by them in Judge Benderthorp's chambers, explaining how they'd helped get the drug dealers off the streets.

Judge Benderthorp lectured them about the danger they'd put Detective Murphy and themselves in. He also reminded them of the extensive court costs, but shook their hands when they left.

"Don't expect to be popular at your school," Detective Murphy warned them. "You won't be. Not even straight kids believe in telling on someone, not even on a drug dealer. It's a stupid kid code, but it's effective. You may feel isolated for a while, but hang in there."

"We can weather it okay," Mike told him.

"We still have each other," Nita added, grinning shyly at Mike.

After they left police headquarters, they stopped off at Mr. Kroeger's apartment. "Mr. Kroeger," Mike said. "I want to apologize for the terrible mess. I guess I never appreciated what good journalism means until I offended it so badly."

"Correction—we both want to apologize," Nita said.

"Apologies won't be enough for the principal," Mr. Kroeger said. "But he isn't entirely without heart. He's arranged for you to spend a week in detention—that means you will still be in school, but you won't be in your regular classes. You'll be in disciplinary class instead. So you won't miss any work and your grades won't be affected. It's something new they've come up with to deal with truants. Oh, and you're both suspended from the newspaper staff for the rest of the semester—sorry."

He rubbed his stomach gingerly. "I am on probation at school myself."

He scowled. "I have apologies to make, too. I had just about forgotten the true meaning of good journalism myself. I so filled your heads with stories of clandestine reporting that I mislead you about journalism, I'm afraid. Then by the time you kids told me the truth I'd gotten so caught up in fighting for the right to protect sources I'd lost track of what real journalism is all about. It's telling the

126

truth, kids. The pure and simple truth. Don't ever forget it."

He shook his head, staring at his feet. "I was wrong to talk you kids into getting those school records, er, irregularly, and defying hospital rules. I put you both in real danger—to boost my own sense of importance. I guess I had the idea that I could somehow make up to journalism for the way I've failed it. I had some delusion that I could just wear down the judge until he quit asking for my sources. I thought I could help set an important legal precedent for newspapers. I wanted to make a real contribution, you see."

Mr. Kroeger sighed wearily. "I suppose it will be up to some future court to make the final decision about the question of confidentiality. I should never have tried to use you two as extensions of myself. I guess I'm like a parent who never could play baseball but is determined to see that my kid is player of the year. You see, I never really—"

"Mr. Kroeger," Mike interrupted, guessing that Mr. Kroeger was about to tell them the true story about his past, "I think all of us have learned a lot about journalism—and ourselves—from this experience."

Mr. Kroeger lifted an eyebrow. He seemed to understand what Mike was telling him.

Their teacher grinned broadly. "See you in school,

Monday. And—be on time to those detention classes, will you?"

The three of them shook hands, sealing an understanding.

"Why don't you come home with me, Mike, and have some lemonade. I could go for a tall glass, couldn't you?" Nita said.

"Your house?" Mike asked.

"I—I feel the need to share a little family history with you."

Mike reached over to touch her hand. "Nita, remember this: nothing you can say about your family will change our friendship. Because it isn't your family or where you live that makes me like you. Okay?"

"Okay," Nita said, grinning shyly. "But I want to—need to—talk. Real friends level with each other, don't they?"

Mike grinned. "Ready when you are, Rapunzel!"